1

I am hidden on the other side of the door, I listen, and she says that several hours after what the copy of the report I keep twice-folded in my drawer calls the *attempted homicide*, and which I call the same thing for lack of a better word, since no other term is more appropriate for what happened, which means I always have the anxious nagging feeling that my story, whether told by me or whomever else, begins with a falsehood, I left my apartment and went downstairs.

I crossed the street in the rain so I could wash my sheets on the hot setting at the launderette down the street, just fifty metres from the door to my building, I was bent double, the laundry bag was so big and heavy my legs trembled under its weight.

It wasn't yet light out. The street was empty. I was alone and as I stumbled along, though I had such a short way to go, I found myself counting in my haste: *Just fifty more steps, keep going, just twenty more steps and you're there.*

I hurried faster. In my impatience for the future, which would, somehow or other, dispatch, consign, reduce this scene to the past, I found myself thinking: *In a week you'll say, It's been a whole week since it happened, keep going, and in a year you'll say, It's been a whole year since it happened.* The drops of freezing rain weren't beating down but fell in a thin, clammy drizzle that soaked through the canvas of my shoes, the water oozed its way through my insoles and the fabric of my socks. I was cold – and I thought: *He could come back, he's bound to come back, now I can never go home, he's driven me from my home.* The manager of the launderette was on duty, his blocky chest and head looming up across the rows of machines. He asked how it was going, I said *Bad*, in the hardest voice I could muster. I waited for him to say something. I wanted him to say something. But he let it go, he shrugged, he turned and disappeared into the little office of his, tucked away behind the dryers, and I hated him for not asking what I meant.

I went back with the clean sheets. I climbed the stairs in a sweat. I remade the bed, but still it smelled like Reda, so I lit candles, I burned incense; it wasn't enough; I took air freshener, deodorant, bottles of cologne that I'd been given for my last birthday, aftershave, and I sprayed the sheets, I soaked the pillowcases, even though I'd just washed them, until the material foamed with thick clustering suds. I washed the wooden chairs with soap and water, took a damp sponge to the books he'd

ÉDOUARD LOUIS

Édouard Louis is the author of *The End of Eddy*, *History of Violence* and *Who Killed My Father*, and the editor of a book on the social scientist Pierre Bourdieu. His work has appeared in the *New York Times*, the *Guardian* and *Freeman's*. His books have been translated into thirty languages and have made him one of the most celebrated writers of his generation.

ALSO BY ÉDOUARD LOUIS

The End of Eddy
Who Killed My Father

ÉDOUARD LOUIS

History of Violence

TRANSLATED FROM THE FRENCH BY
Lorin Stein

VINTAGE

1 3 5 7 9 10 8 6 4 2

Vintage
20 Vauxhall Bridge Road,
London SW1V 2SA

Vintage is part of the Penguin Random House group of companies
whose addresses can be found at global.penguinrandomhouse.com

Penguin
Random House
UK

First published in Vintage in 2019
First published in hardback by Harvill Secker in 2018
First published with the title *Histoire de la violence* in
France by Éditions du Seuil in 2016

penguin.co.uk/vintage

A CIP catalogue record for this book is available from the British Library

ISBN 9781784706074

This book is supported by the Institut français (Royaume-Uni)
as part of the Burgess programme.

INSTITUT
FRANÇAIS
ROYAUME-UNI

Printed and bound in Great Britain by Clays Ltd, Elcograf S.p.A.

Excerpts from *Sanctuary* by William Faulkner, published by Vintage
Classics, and *Kaddish for an Unborn Child* by Imre Kertész, translated
by Tim Wilkinson, published by Vintage and reproduced by permission
of The Random House Group Ltd. © 2010.

The translator wishes to thank Scott Auerbach, Tash Aw, John McGhee
and the author for their good counsel. Any errors are his own.

Penguin Random House is committed to a sustainable future
for our business, our readers and our planet. This book is made
from Forest Stewardship Council® certified paper.

For Geoffroy de Lagasnerie

handled, rubbed the doorknobs with antiseptic wipes, dusted the wooden blinds slat by slat, moved and rearranged the stacks of books on the floor, polished the metal bed frame, scoured the smooth white refrigerator door with lemon-scented detergent; I couldn't stop, I was possessed by an almost manic energy. I thought: *Better crazy than dead.* I scrubbed the shower he'd used, dumped several litres of bleach into the toilet and sink (it was two litres at least – a bottle and a half), scrubbed the entire bathroom, it was absurd, I even cleaned the mirror where he'd observed, or really admired, his reflection the night before, and I threw away the clothes he'd touched, washing them wasn't good enough; I don't know why it was good enough for the sheets but not the clothes. I got down on my hands and knees and scrubbed the floor, the steaming water scalded my fingers, the cloth tore the tender skin away in little oblong strips. The bits of skin curled up on themselves. I paused, I took deep breaths, the truth is I was sniffing like an animal, I had become an animal, sniffing after the scent that seemed never to disappear, no matter what I did, his smell wouldn't go away, so I decided it must be on me, not on the sheets or the furniture. I was the problem. I got in the shower, I washed myself once, twice, three times, and so on. I lathered my body with soap, shampoo, conditioner to perfume it as best I could, it was as if his smell were encrusted inside me, between the flesh and the epidermis, and I scraped at every inch of my body with my nails, I sanded away in a fury, trying to reach the inner layers of my skin and get rid of his smell, I swore out loud, 'Fuck,' and the longer the smell persisted, the sicker and dizzier I felt. Then I realised: *The smell is inside my nose. You're smelling the inside of your nose. The smell is stuck in my nose.* I left the bathroom, came back with saline, and squirted it into my nostrils; I exhaled as if I were blowing my nose so that – this was the effect I wanted to produce – the saline would get to the entire inner surface of my nostrils; it didn't do any good; I left the windows open and went to go see Henri, the only friend I had who was awake that 25 December at nine or ten in the morning.

My sister is the one describing this scene to her husband. I still recognise her voice even after my years away, her voice compounded, as always, of fury, resentment, irony too, and resignation:

'But that's the thing, it didn't surprise me at all and that's exactly what got me so mad, because when he told me – and he was sitting right there where you are now, and here I was listening, he always goes on about how nobody listens to him, which I mean, please, that's not the problem, the problem is he never wants anyone else to talk, only him and he never stops, but as I was saying, when he told me how he left the hospital that day and it hit me how he never called me the day it happened, I said to myself: Of course not – but I kept my mouth shut, and at first I just sat there and dealt with it. I dealt with it. I was proud of the way I dealt with it, actually. I patted myself on the back. And I told myself, You knew who you were dealing with, did you really think he'd pick up the phone or, heaven forbid, come to visit *(here it comes)*. I'm not saying he should have called me before he called everybody else or told me everything in detail right then and there, it's not like I want to be the first person he calls, I'm not saying call and spend three hours on the phone, or three days, not at all. All I'm saying is call.

'But so I let him talk. I dig my nails into my hands, deep, to keep from bawling him out. I could see the big veins come up on my hands while he went on talking, I was clenching them so hard, they looked like beetroots, and all that time, the whole entire time, I was swallowing my spit to swallow the words I felt rising up in my throat, and I just kept telling myself: Hold it together, Clara. Hold it together.

'And finally I told him. Édouard, I mean. I told all this to my mother yesterday, he says he doesn't want to see her but so what, that's between them, it's not my problem. Let them fight *(that's not true, she's lying to him, in fact she has tried desperately to make peace between you, she's done everything she could think of, everything, just the way your mother would try to make peace in her own family, as if the role had been passed down from one to the other)*. I called her to tell her how he's doing, and I told her, I said, Oh my, you should have seen how it all came out, it just came out all by itself while Édouard was talking – it really is stronger than I am, I told her, but Maman, you know how I am, I've always had to say what's on my mind, and it's too late to change now, I'm too old, I've been around for a quarter of a century, and that's not the way I do things, it just isn't, I don't care if he wants to harp on bad memories, that doesn't mean I have to shut up, no way, I won't put up with that kind of blackmail. I'm sorry, I told her, but no, because if you give in to that kind of blackmail then you don't say anything, and that means you stop ever talking about anything and you're always biting your tongue about something and that's no way to live, so I told my mother what I said to Édouard: You could at least have tried, it wouldn't have been that hard, for Christ sake, you could have done it, you could have called me that day. It's not exactly complicated, is it, it's not like you're a righty with two left hands, you do know how to work a goddamn phone. To think it's been almost a year since it happened and he only told me this week. That for a whole year I didn't know anything about it, not until this week.

'And I didn't even mention that she asked him while he was there at the hospital. The nurse, I mean. I know this for a fact. She leaned towards him – she was good at her job and knew what to do, she was a good person, he told me so himself. She leaned towards him and she said, Do you want to contact your family? Do you have any family somewhere you ought to contact? – and what does he say, all calm like it's nothing: No, no, thank you, that's okay. And so he was sitting there yesterday right where you're sitting now. He was practically in the same position and then he imitated himself the way he told the nurse: No, no, thank you, that's okay, and that's why I gave him a dirty look, because I wanted him to know how I felt. And then I thought: I'm more than a quarter century old. We're practically the same age. I've known him for almost a quarter of a century and he hasn't changed a bit *(but also, as soon as you arrived she started talking, non-stop, without listening to anything you said, telling you all the trivial gossip of the village, describing all the weddings and funerals of people whose names you don't even remember, as if that way she could give herself the illusion, and give you the illusion, that you'd never left, that these stories still concerned you and that she was picking up a conversation that the two of you had only just abandoned, a day or an hour before. And so you decided to take your revenge).'*

I showed up at her house four days ago. I'd told myself, naïvely, that time in the country was what I needed in order to get over the weariness and passivity that had consumed my life, but no sooner had I walked through the door, thrown my bag down on the bed, and opened the bedroom window, with its view of the woods and the factory in the next village, than I knew it was a mistake and that I'd go home feeling even worse than before, even more depressed by my own inertia.

It's been two years since my last visit. When she

complains about how long I've been away, I mumble some empty cliché like 'I need to make a life of my own' and try to sound as if I mean it, as if it were her fault, not mine.

But really I have no idea what I'm doing here. The last time I came, she picked me up in the same car, with the same sickening smell of old tobacco, and as I watched the same fields roll by on the other side of the door – the corn and rapeseed, the same reeking acres of sugar beet, the rows of brick houses, the loathsome National Front posters, the grim little churches, the abandoned petrol stations, the rusted-out, falling-down supermarkets surrounded by pasture, the depressing landscape of northern France – I was overcome by a wave of nausea. I'd realised that it would make me lonely. By the time I left, I told myself I hated the country and I swore I'd never come back. And now here I am again. *And there's another reason you stayed away. Not just because you always start fighting the minute you show up*, I thought when I arrived, when I was in her car, when I was singing so we wouldn't have to talk, *not just because you experience everything about her – how she acts, the things she does, the way she thinks – as a personal attack, as an affront. You've also stayed away because you've discovered how easy it is to cut her loose, how little you actually miss her, and sometimes you rub her face in it because you want her help, because you want her to help you leave. Now she knows. She knows how cold you can be and you're ashamed. Even if there's no reason to be ashamed, even if you have every right to cut her loose, still you're ashamed. You know that coming to see her means facing your own cruelty, what in your shame you call your cruelty. To see her is to see a side of yourself you don't like, and that makes you resent her. You can't help it.*

Since my last visit, all I've sent is a few text messages and a few perfunctory postcards, pictures chosen at random out of some vague sense of familial obligation. She's stuck them to her fridge with magnets, each postcard hastily scribbled from a park bench or a table in some café ('Kisses from Barcelona, See you soon, Édouard' or 'Thinking of you in Rome, beautiful weather'), maybe less to keep up our connection – which is what I tell myself – than to remind her of the distance between us, to make her understand we'll never be close again.

Her husband is home from work. From where I'm standing, I can just see his feet. He and Clara are in the parlour, I'm in the next room. With the door ajar, I can hear whatever they say, but they can't see me hiding here rigid behind the door. I can't see them either – except for his feet – but my ears tell me she's sitting in the chair on the other side of the room. He listens, motionless, and she speaks.

'He told me straight out he hardly knew a thing about the man, except his first name was Reda.'

Didier and Geoffroy say he was lying, they say he gave me a made-up name. For all I know, they're right. But I refuse to believe it, each time the thought occurs to me I bat it away. I focus on something else, as if, after all he took away, I want him to leave me that much, as if my knowing those four letters could bring a kind of revenge or, if *revenge* is too strong a word, at least a kind of power over him, a power derived from knowledge. I don't want to lose that, too. Whenever I tell this story and I hear someone say that, obviously, he didn't give me his real name, when I'm told it's textbook to use a fake name in a case like this, in this kind of situation, it always touches a nerve, I can't help getting angry, I can't stand to hear it, I want to shout the person down, to shut them up, to shake them.

'He told me the story again this morning. We were at the bakery and I asked to hear it all again,' and it's true, on the way to the bakery I told her that when Reda pointed his gun at me – because that was the part she wanted to hear over and over again – when he pointed his gun at me, the question I asked myself wasn't *Is he going to kill me?* because by then there was no doubt in my mind, it was already over, he was going to kill me and I was going to die, that very night, in my own room, I accepted it the way one accepts and adapts to any situation; for as history shows, people do adjust and adapt, even to the most inhumane conditions, even in the face of atrocities, and this – I told Clara, giving in to my weakness for grandiosity – is both the best and the worst news for humanity, since it means all you have to change is the world and then people will change themselves, or at least most people, and (Clara wasn't listening) there's no need to change them person by person, which would take forever; people adapt, they don't endure, they adapt. So the question wasn't *Is he going to kill me?* but *How is he going to kill me?* In other words: *Is he going to wrap his scarf around my neck again and strangle me?* or *Is he going to take a dirty knife out of the sink?* or *Is he going to pull the trigger of his gun?* or *Will he find a way I can't even imagine?* I'd stopped looking for ways to escape, I'd stopped hoping to survive, all I wanted was to die as painlessly as possible. Later on the police, or maybe it was Clara, congratulated me on my bravery, and the idea of bravery struck me as utterly out of place, as alien to that night. He takes a few steps back, gripping the butt of his gun. He stretches out his other hand, the empty one, and without ever looking down, he reaches into the pile of clothes on my chair, he feels around. He pulls out the scarf. I think: *He's going to strangle me again.* But when he came near me, he didn't try to strangle me the way he had a few minutes before, before he took out his gun. He didn't reach for my neck. This time he tried to tie me up, he was holding on to my right arm and trying to grab the other arm so he could tie the scarf around it, I remember he smelled of sweat and also of sex. I fought back, I held him off, and I was so afraid I thought: *I don't want to die*, or something just as tragically clichéd. I cried out, but softly; obviously I didn't make too much noise. I couldn't risk it. I pushed him away, very calmly, as calmly as I could. *Don't do that*, I pleaded. I struggled, I fought him off, and all the while he kept repeating the same thing, louder and louder, *I'm going to take care of your ass I'm going to take care of your ass* (*take care of* not in the usual sense, but rather in the sense of 'deal with', that is, in this context, *destroy*) *I'm going to take care of your ass I'm going to take care of your ass.* Now he was shouting. I hoped a neighbour would hear us and call the police. *But if the police come, what if he's so afraid of getting arrested that he panics and kills me when he hears them calling, 'Police, open up,' through the door?* When he couldn't manage to tie me up, he took out the gun, which he'd stashed in the inside pocket of his fake leather jacket, he threw his scarf on the floor or else he put it around his neck, I can't remember which, and he shoved me down on the bed.

The morning of the twenty-fifth, just a few hours after this scene, I walked and biked to my friend Henri's, and on my way there I was still thinking, *In a week you'll tell yourself: It's been a whole week since it happened, keep going, and in a year you'll tell yourself: It's been a whole year since it happened.* I'd just reached his landing when he opened the door. He must have heard my feet on the stairs. I wanted to throw myself into his arms and yet I hesitated, though I couldn't have said why.

I told Clara, 'It wasn't that I thought he might be dangerous.' In the very beginning, right after my night with Reda, I didn't yet believe – as I would believe for months, later on – that anyone could turn dangerous, even the people I was closest to, that they might turn homicidal, and be seized by a lust for blood and destruction and simply attack me, even Didier and Geoffroy, my two closest friends; and yet face-to-face with Henri something held me back. We both froze, and in those few seconds, while time stood still, I could feel him gently scrutinising and analysing, searching for any clue that could explain what I was doing there, so early, on such an unlikely day. His eyes swept over me, they took in my dirty, greasy hair, the dark rings around my eyes, my neck with its constellation of purple marks, my crimson swollen lips. As he took it all in, his face collapsed by degrees; I remember the many showers I took before I went to Henri's, and yet I very distinctly remember my hair was dirty when I got there. He invited me in. He followed behind me, and I could feel his gaze on the back of my neck. I wasn't crying. I made my way inside. His tables were covered with framed photos, and over the sofa there was a big portrait of him, behind glass. I sat down and Henri made coffee. He came back from the kitchen holding two cups, they were rattling in their saucers; he asked if I wanted to tell him what happened, I said yes. I described Reda, first his brown eyes and black eyebrows; I began with his eyes. His face was smooth. His features were soft yet rugged, masculine. When he smiled, he had dimples, and he smiled a lot. The copy of the report that I keep at home, drafted in police language, refers to an *Arab male*. Each time I see that phrase it infuriates me, because I can still hear the racism of the police who interviewed me later, on that 25 December, I can hear the compulsive racism that, in the end, seemed the crucial bond between them, the only bond they had – apart from their too-tight uniforms – the only glue that held them together, because for them *Arab* didn't refer to somebody's geographical origins, it meant scum, criminal, thug. At the police station I'd given a brief description of Reda, when they asked, and immediately the officer on duty cut me off: 'Oh, you mean he was an Arab.' He was triumphant, *delighted* would be an exaggeration, but he did smile, he crowed; it was as if I'd given him the confession he'd wanted to hear since I walked in the door, as if I'd given him proof that he was in the right all along; he kept repeating it, 'the Arab male, the Arab male', every other sentence involved 'the Arab male'. I told Henri about my night and went to lie down on his bed. He pointed me to his bedroom, in the loft, and I climbed up and went to sleep. I hadn't slept in a long time, apart from a few naps with Reda.

2

My sister goes on with her monologue, I can hear her sip her water, swallow, set her glass on the table; I can hear the clack of glass on plywood.

'And that was what surprised him the most, he told me, he says: The next day I woke up and it started. Just like that *(I told her I was lying on my bed, lying on my back, and when I opened my eyes my entire body went into a cramp, it felt as if there were blades between my ribs, my back stiffened like a shell)*, and what's his reaction, right then and for days after? That he'll never be able to see anybody happy ever again. The moron. I don't remember his exact words, but that was the gist. What could I say? I just kept my mouth shut, I looked down at my shoes like I was a moron too *(I tried to go back to sleep, I wanted to sleep, but my body hurt too much)*. And he says to me, I hated everyone, I know it's crazy, Clara, but that morning I woke up hating everyone *(and I thought: How can you hate them?)*.

'Which was a weird thing to say, if you ask me. I

wouldn't call it exactly normal. But there it was. In my head I'm thinking, *Get a grip*, but I don't say it out loud, he'd only take it the wrong way. He said, I hated everyone *(and I thought: How can you hate them? That morning after Reda left, I woke up and my mouth tasted strange – and I was thinking I'd never be able to bear the slightest trace or sign or appearance of what people call happiness, if I'd seen someone smiling I would have slapped them, I'd have grabbed them by the lapels, I'd have shaken them as hard as I could, and I'd have shouted in their face, I'd have screamed; even children, even children, the frail or the sick, I'd have wanted to shake them and spit in their faces, I'd have scratched until I drew blood, I'd have scratched their faces off, till all the faces around me disappeared. I would have stuck my fingers into their eyes, gouged out their eyes and crushed them in my hand, and I thought: How can you hate them? and it wasn't my fault, I would have grabbed the sick ones, lifted them up and thrown them out of their wheelchairs, my god, I could never see another smile or hear anyone laugh, outside, in the street, in the park, wherever I was the laughter pierced my eardrums and stuck in my ears, it echoed inside my skull for the rest of the day, it stuck in my skull, in my eyes, in my lips – it was as if their laughter existed to hurt me).*

'So what could he do? The trouble was he couldn't even go outside and clear out the cobwebs, with the shitty weather they were having *(I could hear the patter of the rain on the windows, it was raining, it had been raining the entire month of January)*. He tried to go back to sleep but he was in too much pain from the cramps, all he could do was keep replaying what had happened. He couldn't tell what was what. It was kind of like when you go to sleep and wish you could wake up the next day and be somebody else, like you were changed – only he hadn't wished it, anyway not like that.

'And he felt the same even when it wasn't real *(even when it wasn't real)*. Even when he saw ads on the bus or on the walls of some building, when he saw all the photos of happy families eating breakfast or sitting by a pool, you know what I mean, when he saw what they call happiness in advertisements, he wanted to take out a knife or something, he wanted to take a key out of his pocket and tear up the faces *(I wanted to light them on fire)*. He wanted to drag them down with him, as many as he could, that's what he told me *(I told her: to spread the pain)*. And he told me: I know it doesn't make any sense *(I thought: How can you hate them? but it wasn't just when I saw them smile, I told her I couldn't stand to see unhappy faces either, it was as if their unhappiness were less authentic, less true, less profound, less real than my own)*.

'It's true she used to tell us lots of stories like that, our mother did. Maybe it did something to him, hearing those stories over and over back when he still lived at home. Who knows. The other day on Channel Two a man was saying how if a person never heard anyone talk about love maybe they wouldn't be able to fall in love. Which, I mean, please. When I hear myself say it, I tell myself enough with the TV, it's frying your brain. But even so. It's been on my mind.

'It started when she was doing the home care for the elderly, before I knew you. Oh, don't you let anyone give you that line, about how it's a job with a future as long as people keep getting old. She'd wash them and then she'd give them their medication – and then she'd come home and complain. My god, they never gave her a moment's peace. But if you're a woman what can you do? Especially now they've stopped hiring at the factory, everything's gone, and now they're saying it'll close for good.'

And it was worse than she lets on, it was harder than she said, because our mother didn't have a driver's licence and she had to compete with all the other women – and there were a lot of them – who wanted the work just as badly, partly to bring home a pay cheque, partly just to get away from their husbands. She had to fight to get that job, when by a miracle they were hiring, she took her bicycle, which she got fixed especially for the occasion, and she rode it from one office to another, she dressed up and she pinned up her hair and she took time with her make-up, and put on a little more than usual even though our father didn't like that and he'd scold her or even forbid it, 'You look better without it,' 'That crap is for whores,' and she would go back and knock on those office doors, and she kept going back, again and again, even when they told her no, even when she thought it was a lost cause, even when she felt it slipping through her fingers, she kept going back just to show how determined she was; she'd go back in the rain or snow, always on her bike, she'd send letter after letter, she'd call on the phone to say she was worried when she hadn't had any word. And it worked, for a few years that's what she did. She'd come home and tell us how, out of what must be some animal instinct, the old people whose houses she cleaned would descend into unspeakable behaviour, as if they wanted to take their death out on everyone around them, as if they were willing to face death as long as they could leave behind some nasty souvenir of their existence; they'd break everything in the house; they'd pull the tablecloth off the table, smash the souvenirs on the floor, throw the dishes against the walls.

'And every day it was the same thing all over again. Every day there'd be knick-knacks flying every which way, picture frames, snow globes from Lourdes, place mats they'd picked up on holiday. They crushed, they just shattered everything. You've never heard anything like the shit they'd yell in our mother's face, you never have and you never will, some of it you carry with you and never forget, oh, even the women who used to call themselves ladies and go around with their noses in the air. Don't kid yourself, they weren't any better than the rest. Those ones are the dirtiest of all because finally for once in their lives they can let themselves go. They'd go shouting their dirty songs, *It's Dudule's giant dick*, *The slut's going to wash your filthy ass*, I swear, and then other days, the bad days, they'd do their business all over their own damn house, my mother told me, on the kitchen table, on the floor, everywhere. They'd just have at it while she was there on her knees, doing her best to bathe their flabby, crumply old arses and them sitting there in a living-room chair and her with nothing but a scratchy old bath glove and a cheap plastic basin, their bodies so flabby it was like they were overflowing and melting right into the chair. And when our mother got home she'd be in tears after her day at work. She couldn't take it any more. She would cry: She just shat everywhere, old Madame Millard, and she wiped with the dining-room curtains — I can't take it any more, how long can I go on? She told us, There was shit all over, I had to clean it up and you know I can't stand the smell of shit, it's always disgusted me, more than anything there is, I never could stand the smell of shit and I still can't. I thought I'd hurl, I held it in but it was all I could do not to throw up everywhere, all over everything and then just leave and never go back — and we'd say, Don't worry, Mother, the next heatwave will take care of them. That would calm her down. And so with Édouard — not that he's as badly off as they were, I don't mean to say he is — but for a long time after that Christmas he'd have these nervous breakdowns of his, when he wanted to drag everyone down with him, like those old ladies our mother took care of. And he told me: It got harder every day. In the end he decided to just stay home, all by himself, he never left the house. He closed the blinds. He locked himself in. He put his hands over his ears and he'd press them tight so he wouldn't hear the neighbours' voices coming through the walls or the handyman having his conversations in the courtyard.'

On my calmer days I imagined going up to a stranger in some public place, on the street or in the aisles of a supermarket, and telling the entire story from beginning to end. The way I imagined it, I would walk up, the stranger would be startled, and I'd start talking, as casually as if I'd known him all my life, without ever saying my name, and what I'd tell him would be so ugly he'd have no choice but to stand there and listen till the end; he would listen, and I would watch his face. I spent my time dreaming up scenes where I did this. I didn't tell Clara, but this fantasy of utter shamelessness and self-exposure sustained me for weeks.

The reality was I couldn't stop talking about it. Within a week after Christmas, I had told the story to most of my friends, but not just to my friends; I had also repeated it to people I wasn't close to, acquaintances or people I'd hardly met, sometimes people I only knew on Facebook. I bristled if they tried to respond, if they tried to empathise or give me their analysis of what had happened, as for example when Didier and Geoffroy suggested that

Reda wasn't his actual name. I wanted everyone to know my story, but I wanted to be the only one among them who possessed the truth of what had happened, and the more I told the story, the more I talked about it, the more I felt that I was the only person, the only one, who knew what had really happened – this in stark contrast to the laughable naïveté of everyone around me. No matter what the conversation was, I found a way of bringing it back to Reda, of dragging him back in, of connecting everything to him, as if every topic of conversation must *logically* lead to my memory of what he'd done.

The first week of February – barely a month after Christmas – I went to meet an author who had sent a note inviting me to lunch. I didn't know him, but I accepted the invitation, and I knew why. He wanted me to write a piece for the special issue of a journal he was editing (the piece I turned in a few days later was very bad, for obvious reasons), and I behaved as I've just described. In those days the words I spoke were not quite my own. The author walked into the restaurant where I was waiting for him, already quivering in my chair, fiddling with the pencil eraser I'd found in my pocket; he sat down, he took off his jacket, he reached to shake my hand, and no sooner was he in his chair than my lips were burning to tell him about Christmas. I thought: *No, you can't start in on it yet. Give it a moment. At least pretend to talk about something else.* Outside, the grey-blue of the sky was reflected in the glass facades of the buildings; I remember this not because I care about the sky but because I wasn't listening and I was looking out of the window, distracted and bored, whenever it wasn't my turn to talk.

We exchanged a few words and for maybe ten minutes I held my breath, feeling that I might explode if I didn't say Reda's name. I contained myself, I pretended to be having the sort of conversation people like us would normally have, I played my part, I got the author to talk about his work, his books, his projects, but I wasn't listening. I didn't listen to a word he said. And when it was my turn, I answered his questions without listening to my answers; what made it even harder to maintain control was that everything he said, everything he made me say, every observation he made sounded like a roundabout invitation to talk about Christmas. Which is to say, I created connections everywhere, everything I perceived and therefore my entire construction of reality was conditioned by Reda. And whenever I opened my mouth, I was afraid that the words *Reda* or *Christmas* would come out, too soon, against my will.

Then I spoke. I decided it was time, I thought: *I've held back long enough, now you've earned the right*, and I did what I'd been waiting to do since he walked into the restaurant: I monopolised the conversation, I held the floor for the entire remainder of our lunch and he said nothing, apart from a few brief comments between mouthfuls of food: 'How terrible,' 'What a nightmare,' 'My god,' etc., which only added to my jubilation. At the end of the meal I begged him not to repeat anything I'd said; what's more, I didn't know why I'd gone into all that, and for this too I apologised, for this too I excused myself, why had I gone into all that when I hardly knew him, how could I have been so inappropriate – for I realised what I'd done – how could I have been so inappropriate, how could I have been so rude? And this was more or less the way I existed, spoke, acted in the weeks after the attack.

The manic talking had started at the hospital. It was an hour or two after Reda left, I had hurried to the closest emergency room to get a dose of antiretrovirals. The hospital was nearly empty that morning of 25 December; a homeless man was pacing back and forth in the waiting room. He wasn't waiting for anything, he was just there to get out of the cold. He said, 'Merry Christmas, monsieur,' when I sat down a few feet away. This *Merry Christmas, monsieur*, so incongruous, so odd in that setting and after what I'd been through, made me burst out laughing. I was seized by a fit of insane, helpless laughter that echoed, loud and jarring, through the empty waiting room, I can still hear my terrible laughter bouncing off the walls; I was doubled over, holding my stomach with both hands, I couldn't breathe, and between shouts of laughter I answered, out of breath: 'Thank you, monsieur, thank you, Merry Christmas to you, too.'

I waited. But nobody came. So I sat there. I felt like an extra in somebody else's story. I tried desperately to remember, to ward off the idea, not that nothing had happened – that would have been out of the question – but that the whole thing had happened to someone else, to some other person, and that I had observed the scene from outside; I thought: *That's where this obsession comes from. That's why you're always asking what your childhood self would think of the adult you've become.* I thought: *You've always felt your life was happening somewhere else, in spite of you, and that you were just a spectator, you never recognised your life as your own. It's nothing new. When you were little and your parents took you to the supermarket you'd watch the people go by with their shopping trolleys. You'd stare at them, you did this as long as you could remember, you used to look at their clothes, the way they walked, and you'd say to yourself: I want to be like this one, I don't want to be like that one. And you would never have imagined becoming the person you are today. Never. Not even as a thing you didn't want.*

I craned my neck so I could look out of the windows of the waiting room, just to pass the time. Time dragged. I waited for one of the security doors to open, I waited for a doctor to appear, I coughed, I sniffled, I pressed the red button of the little buzzer on the reception desk, and after twenty or thirty minutes of waiting a nurse appeared. That's when the talking mania began. At least, that anyone could notice. I had already had to restrain myself from talking to the homeless guy, who was obviously drunk, after his *Merry Christmas*, and I had to actively keep from telling him that what he'd said was ironic since here I was at the hospital on 25 December, that is, on a day when we ought to have been somewhere else, him and me both – and I held back from telling him all about what had brought me there, to the emergency room. But now I didn't hold back, and when the nurse asked how he could help me – actually, I think he probably wasn't a nurse but maybe an orderly, or an intake person, or a switchboard operator – I told him everything. I didn't restrain my tears. I didn't even try, I was convinced that if I didn't cry he wouldn't believe me. Not that my tears were put on, the pain was real. But I also knew I'd have to act the part or no one would believe me.

This worry of mine seems to have grown in the days that followed. Later, in another hospital, when I was determined to win a doctor's sympathy, to make him understand and believe me, my voice remained flat and metallic, I sounded cold and distant, my eyes were dry. I had already cried too much, I had nothing left to give. You'd better cry or he won't believe you, I thought, you need to cry. My eyes had become the eyes of a stranger. I tried to force myself. I strained to produce tears, I called up images of Reda, his face, the gun, but nothing happened, no tears, try as I might they wouldn't form, they wouldn't pool in the corners of my eyes, it was hopeless, they were as dry as ever, I was just as calm as when I'd walked in, and the doctor behind his glasses nodded his head, his glasses shone on his nose.

I thought back on other scenes from my life. I dredged up other bad memories, the saddest and most painful I had, anything to make myself cry. I remembered when I heard the news that Dimitri was dead.

Didier had called in the middle of the night to tell me; I was out walking, it was late, I was alone and first my phone had rung and vibrated in my pocket. It was Didier sending me a text to ask 'Can I call you?'; and right away I feared the worst, why would he ask if he could call instead of just calling? I was afraid something had happened to Geoffroy, that maybe he'd been in an accident. I was trying not to think of his body laid out on a stretcher – it was the first thought I had – and I wrote back: 'Yes of course,' already trembling, my fingers shaking as they slid across the screen.

My mobile rang a second time, I hesitated before I picked up, then Didier told me, his voice controlled but wavering too, wavering out of its forced artificial calm, that Dimitri, who'd had a big meeting far from Paris, and to whom I'd spoken on the phone just hours before, was dead.

I tried to make myself burst into sobs so the doctor would believe me, but the memory was too old, it didn't touch me any more. I was forcing myself to cry, he looked as sceptical as ever; if only these two opposing forces – my wish to cry and his scepticism – could come together, I thought, we could reach – no, we could establish – the truth; the truth lay in the clash between my wish and his scepticism, in the tension between them. No matter how hard I tried, I couldn't do it.

But there, that first evening, with the orderly at the first hospital, I cried easily enough. He was reassuring: 'Someone's going to take care of you, someone who can help you better than I can,' at which point I almost screamed, 'I don't think you understand.' Finally the nurse arrived. When she came up to me and asked what had brought me there, I talked, and talked some more, and went on talking.

Now that's all over. I behave differently now. Instead of trying to say everything, nowadays I realise I'm always short of breath, I feel tired and indifferent; I'm depleted, and that's the reason I got on the train and came to Clara's. Certain fears still rise up from time to time, fears I try not to name. Yesterday, for example, we were on our way back from a walk in the forest, and I told her how, since Christmas, I'd been haunted by a story Cyril told me – I don't know when, it doesn't matter – about people who thought they'd caught AIDS, or who learned they had it, back when the disease first appeared, before there was any treatment. Cyril was walking beside me. There was no treatment at the time, he told me, and these people, when they thought they had it – or knew they had it – expected to die, they expected to die right away, so some of them, he went on – and more than you might think – simply stopped whatever they'd been doing, so they could enjoy however much time they had left, even if it was just a little while. I remember we were on our way home from a party when this came up, it was late, Cyril was walking his bike beside me. They just stopped; since they were about to die, they stopped going through the motions – they stopped doing the chores they had thought of as living, but which now, so close to death, were revealed as chores. They quit their jobs, they left their apartments, they gave up sports, cultural events, their circles of friends. From now on, they said no to every constraint, even little things: no more setting the alarm clock, no more trying to quit smoking or drinking, no more hanging out with people they didn't really like but still hung out with, no more shaking hands with people they actually despised, no more graduation ceremonies or social obligations, no more watching what they ate, no more working for somebody else, no more letting people demean them, use them, no more believing in what everyone said was life, in other words, no more time for any duty that went against their instincts. But then – some of them didn't die; some of these people who thought they were going to die survived. Miraculously, you might say. They'd prepared for death, but death never came. After they'd made their break, Cyril added, most of the survivors never managed to go back to their everyday lives. They couldn't stand the old job, the old apartment, the people they didn't want to see. And ever since my night with Reda, I told Clara, I've been afraid I would have the same reaction, ever since I faced my own death that night with Reda, I've been afraid of not believing, of not believing in anything any more, and of replacing the absurdities of my own life with other absurdities: countryside, rest, simplicity, solitude, reading, water, streams – or even: livestock, barnyards, wood fires – because that's all it would be, replacing one set of absurdities with another; and I thought: *Your being here with Clara means you've failed.*

3

She stops to catch her breath. She says I'd returned my bike three or four hundred metres from my apartment, on the other side of the place de la République. She says I usually returned it to a closer station, but I wanted to walk off some of the wine I'd had with Didier and Geoffroy. I wasn't drunk. I'd had a little more than usual because it was Christmas, a bottle of wine, maybe two, I can't remember, but I wasn't drunk. I was carrying my presents under my arm, two books by Claude Simon – inscribed by Simon to Didier, who had just given them to me – and a volume of Nietzsche's Complete Works including, I remember, *Ecce Homo* and several others, wrapped in brown paper, a present from Geoffroy, who'd got it at the Gallimard bookshop on boulevard Raspail.

'And I'll bet you money he was carrying them right side up, like that, with the cover facing out, so everyone could see what he was reading – you know how people do. Not just that, I can tell you what he was thinking at that moment, on his way home: I've come a hell of a long way. That's what he was telling himself, over and over, because he liked the sound of it, I've come a hell of a long way – and from what? I don't know, from how he grew up, compared with the guys in the village – because he's obsessed with them, they're all he's talked about since he got here – the guys he used to hang around with at the bus stop when they were kids.'

She tells him how she used to watch us ride our bikes in the town hall square, three of us to a bike. I'd be sitting on the handlebars while someone else stood on the pedals, and a third boy would take the seat, and we'd go round and round the square, circling the World War I memorial. Because there were three of us, we couldn't go very fast and the tyres always looked ready to pop against the tarmac. The police would make us cut it out, but then we'd start again, and when she passed by and saw us on the square she used to call out, 'Hey, dickwads, you look like three frogs on a matchstick.' Because, she says, 'I wanted them to know I wasn't like the other girls who were easy and let the boys push them around. The thing with boys is you have to throw the first punch. They're simple like that. For boys the first punch is what counts. You have to be the one that starts it. As long as you throw the first punch, they never mess with you again.'

She tells him how, when we were thirteen or fourteen, she watched us shift our base of operations from the town square to the bus stop. We'd stay out drinking pastis or whisky from plastic cups with the car boot open so we could hear the radio (our neighbour Brian was older than me, he had a driver's licence and a car).

'Anyway, they're the ones he must think about, a lot. One time he even said as much. I was like, It's about time, you idiot. Tell it like it is. It's not like I was surprised. He once told me how, when he comes back to the village and goes to say hi to the guys, the ones he used to play gangsters with at the bus stop like I said, now that it's ten years later he doesn't know what to think. He can't think if he's aged faster than them or the other way round. He told me, We never know how old we are. Because when he sees them there – with their pushchairs, already having families and responsibilities, or some house they're building in the next village, all the things that make you a grown-up, and with him still being at school – it makes him feel like he's twenty years younger, even though they're the exact same age. Because he hasn't got any of that. No house, obviously no wife – good luck with that – no car, no kid, it's like those things belong to another world. He watches, he sees how they've slipped into these grown-up lives of theirs, and how they're never coming back, and he thinks, I'm a baby next to them.

'Other times it's just the opposite. Because he'll be watching them and he'll realise they're all wearing the same clothes they wore when they were kids and they played together, I mean they've got on the same Airness tracksuit Édouard used to wear – my god, how he loved that tracksuit – they've got the same fake Louis Vuitton bags dangling around their necks, they've even got the same jobs, so then he thinks they're the ones who never grew up. Even if they've got kids of their own, you think they've changed? Please. They still hang out, maybe not at the bus stop now, but they hang out in the houses they've built, drinking the same Koenigsbier and saying the same things they used to say when they'd be drinking, That's not beer, that's donkey piss. Suck it down, they'd say, and that's what they did, they sucked it down, they didn't drink, they didn't know how to drink, they never learned how to drink, they only suck it down. They think they're men, but they don't even know how to drink right. They do the same thing every weekend, they talk about girls and they race each other – maybe not on their scooters any more, now they've got cars and can drive, but what's the difference, it's just another pair of wheels. So when Édouard realises that it's all exactly the same, then he feels like he's the one twenty years older and all of a sudden he's ancient – older than twenty anyhow – even though they're all the same age. It makes me feel ancient, those were his words. I'm even ashamed of my body. He stands up straight and he's careful how he walks. He looks at his reflection in car windows to check out the way he's walking, because next to them he thinks he walks like a little old man. He tries to walk younger. Then every time he comes here – and he hardly ever does, god knows what he's got against us – every time he comes here, he goes on about how he can't decide if he's twenty years older or twenty years younger than the kids he grew up with. One day he thinks: Twenty years older, the next day: Twenty years younger. That's why he says you never know your own age.

'So there he was walking along, telling himself, so help me God, I've come a hell of a long way. And when he thinks that way, I know it applies to me, too, at least sometimes. You think in his mind I'm special? Please. He's always reassuring himself, he's always telling himself, I'm different from her now, I've come a long way. I've come a hell of a long way. Honestly, it just kills me – that he could think a thing like that.'

I stand there listening – am I holding still out of concentration and willpower, or have the shame and pain of what she's said left me paralysed, frozen and stiff as the door that stands before me?

'And don't misunderstand me. I'm not saying I blame him. I'm not saying he's done wrong. I've been around, I know we all have thoughts like that. If somebody was to tell me these things never crossed his mind, I'd say they were a liar. Listen, I remember things of my own from time to time. I'll go off by myself just so I can think back on old friends I used to see. I sit in a corner all by myself and I think of them, and I think: You've done all right.

In the end it's the ones I had to get away from, the ones I hated the most, who I think about the most. That's just how it is. I bet it's the same for everyone. You pat yourself on the back, you say, I'm not like them any more, I've made it this far, I must be doing something right. But as I was saying, there he was walking along.'

I never said much about the dinner, only because my memories were so disjointed. I saw us, Geoffroy and me, walking among the Christmas lights in the street, the red and blue bulbs over our heads, with the wind nipping our ears. We were surrounded by people laden down with bags, all I could see were bags instead of bodies, the foot traffic was halting and slow, I couldn't hear any voices, only echoes, snippets, and I loved this crowd in motion, out of clumsiness I stepped on somebody's feet and they laughed it off. Then, next image: we ducked out of line and squeezed our way into an overheated shop to buy tarts. The warmth inside the shop seemed to settle over our cheeks like a radiant second skin; the cold skin stayed cold underneath. Then, next image: Didier is there, there are three of us now. We're sitting down. An hour or so has passed since the scene in the street. I open a bottle of wine. When Didier hears the pop of the cork he laughs and says, 'They're playing my tune,' the expression I taught him, and I laugh too, the laughter fades, Geoffroy serves us pieces of vegetable tart. We start to eat. Then I'm standing, dinner is almost over, I can see the crumbs scattered on the empty plates, Didier is holding out one of the books that are for me, I'm overwhelmed, I read the first words out loud, 'heavy all dressed in black head covered by a black scarf she crossed the deserted beach once she came near the water's edge she sat.' Geoffroy asks me to go on reading, he encourages me, he tells me I'm a good reader. I can't remember whether I did read any more. Then the book has disappeared from my field of vision, I don't know where it is, I can see the computer screen, the computer's on and it's playing songs, arias from an opera but I don't remember which, maybe it was Massenet, the death of Werther, then something else, then something else again, and suddenly we're having dessert, each of us holding a glass, and we're singing, we're singing, we know the arias by heart. Now we're in a different room, now we're propped up on pillows in the bedroom. Then finally, two hours later, the wind is whistling in my ears, the trees are flying by, the streetlights flash across my eyes, the streets are empty. I return the bike to the station at the far end of the place de la République so I can walk.

4

They were doing street work on the place de la République and the ground was covered with mud: or rather
the ground was mud, that's all there was, the torn-up
streets were waiting for the workmen to pour their
cement and turn them into a pedestrian walkway, and
every day I got dirty when I crossed the square, I'd come
home with the bottom of my trousers covered in sandy
dirt. It wasn't the brown, the nearly russet mud I knew
from my country childhood, mud that smelled of fresh
earth and gleamed like clay, mud so clean and whole-
some that you'd happily spread it on your face, this was
the grey, austere, gritty mud of city construction.

On the square there were cranes standing idle, immense
and skeletal, and the entire work site was walled off with
green sheets of metal, which in a matter of days had been
covered with political posters – one I can still see: 'We
won't pay for their crisis, we'll tear capitalism down' –
plus ads and theatre posters, and these metal sheets marked

the borderline between the work already under way and the work that hadn't yet begun.

So: it's Christmas Eve, I'm walking in the dark, I cross the chaos of the place de la République, shoes covered in mud, greyish spatters and droplets on my legs as if it were raining, not from the sky, but from the ground, my Nietzsche and Simon tucked under my arm.

Suddenly I hear a sound behind me.

But I didn't react. I kept walking. And I didn't turn round. And not on purpose either – I just happened not to turn round. The pace of the sounds behind me quickens, coming closer, moving faster, I knew the sounds were coming closer but it didn't occur to me that this phenomenon had anything to do with me, and only when he came up beside me did I identify the sound as his approaching, quickening footsteps. He was the first to speak: 'What's up? You don't do Christmas?'

Reda smiled. He had stopped to my right and was walking now, out of breath. I could see only half his smile and half his face, the other half was in shadow, swallowed up, subsumed by the night. He asked again why I wasn't celebrating Christmas, why I was out so late – and I told Clara I liked the sound of his breathing, I wanted to take his breath in my fingers and spread it all over my face. And yet I said nothing when he smiled.

I don't answer, I keep my head down and try not to look at his half-face; I want to start the books that Didier and Geoffroy just gave me, it was as simple as that. I told my legs to go faster. I kept my mouth shut. I was over-whelmed by his beauty. Clara said, 'To like the way somebody breathes – I mean, really.'

But I'd decided to go home and go to bed, despite his beauty, despite his breath. For strength, I focused on the books in my right hand. I knew I couldn't hold out long. But for a few metres it worked, I managed to ignore him, but my shoulder brushed against his, his footsteps splashed my trousers with grey mud; and I didn't say anything *(Nietzsche Simon Nietzsche Simon)*. He asked, 'What, you don't want to talk?'

I summoned up my memories for the two police offi-cers, a woman and a man, both facing me – him at a computer, her standing beside him. It was less than twenty-four hours after I first met Reda.

The interview had just begun, I was still in the dark. I still had no idea how intensely I would come to hate myself for having gone to the police.

In any case, it was too late for second thoughts. That's what I learned when, in my fatigue and my dismay at the turn the night had taken, I told the police I was hav-ing second thoughts and wanted to go home. The male officer chuckled. It wasn't a cruel laugh, he laughed the way you do when a child says something funny. Then he drew himself up, and he cleared his throat and said, 'I'm sorry, monsieur, but now this is a criminal proceeding. It's out of your hands.' That night I didn't understand how my story could stop belonging to me (which is to say, I was at once excluded from my own story and at the same time forcibly included, because they kept forcing me to talk, over and over again; which is to say, the exclusion and inclusion were one and the same, it could even be argued that the exclusion came first, at least that's how it seemed, since it was through exclusion that my fate was first revealed to me, the fate in which I was now included and from which I was no longer allowed to withdraw).

When I first got there, though, talking was a relief. The two police had welcomed me with compassion, tenderness almost; I kept losing my place, my mind wandered, I said things that in context made no sense, I made a fool of myself, I made stupid pronouncements, I kept coming back to the same thing, the same moment of the night, in different words, in different tones, as if to get at the truth: 'I imagine we'd have looked odd to another person, if they saw him, Reda, I mean, standing there frozen − as if his legs were welded to the ground and reinforced with steel rods that ran down into the earth − and me just sitting there across from him while he strangled me with his scarf, and the wool of the scarf kept squeaking when it tightened around my neck, with that squeaking sound wool makes, it's like nails on a blackboard, and all I could do was sit there, squirming like an earthworm stuck under a shoe, all I could do was twist and turn.' The policeman watched me talk. He wasn't listening, he was watching. His fingers hung over the keyboard he was using to take down my statement. There were long pauses in his typing. His power, I now realised, was above all a power over time; he could drag this interview out or he could end it, he could let the silences linger and harden, he could make me talk, he could rush me or, suddenly, without my even knowing or understanding, he could slow me down. He had asked me to tell him the facts – tell me everything, he said, and don't leave anything out; every minute, every exchange, every word Reda said, however insignificant it might seem, could help them find him and arrest him (and it was exactly the least likely details, he went on, that usually cracked a case, even if – to the untrained and untutored eye – the information seemed meaning-less or non-existent, even if it seemed like nothing).

He asked me: 'Wait - you brought a stranger up to your apartment, in the middle of the night?' I answered: 'But everybody does that . . .' and in an ironic, mocking, sarcastic voice, he asked, 'Everybody?' It wasn't a ques-tion. Obviously, he wasn't asking me whether or not everybody did that, he was saying nobody did that. Or at least, not everybody. So finally I answered, 'What I mean is, people like me . . .' He started to say something else, 'But come on—' when suddenly: 'Stop right there!' The female officer standing beside him ordered him to stop typing. We both jumped. Her 'Stop' was brusque and angry and, at the same time, amused, as if this latest development was merely the final straw, as if she was at her wits' end; it was too late, the harsh glare of the fluorescent lighting was driving her crazy, so was the smell of the floor cleaner, so was the flicker of the computer screens; she couldn't take it seriously any more, her with her hair a mess and the dark rings under her eyes.

Start again, she told us: that's not how you go about it, *in a completely anarchic way* – and I remember how she winced when she said the word *anarchic*. We had to go back to the beginning. 'Tell it in the order that it happened.'

To hold still, I keep my eyes fixed on the door, so I don't give myself away. I study the grain, the branching pathways of dark brown in the light brown wood, and I try to follow the paths as they wander from the centre of the door to its edges, where they disappear.

Clara tells her husband that Reda asked if I was ever going to speak to him. Although I said nothing, clearly he took my silence to mean I couldn't say no. I could hear the smile in his voice but I didn't yet turn to look at him, except furtively – I looked as discreetly as I could, I was still trying to get away, and I thought *Nietzsche, Simon, Nietzsche, Simon, Nietzsche, Simon*. A few steps later, I gave in.

'He gave in, he talked to him.' I told myself I was only responding so he'd leave me alone, but I knew that whatever I was about to say, it would start a conversation.

'He said he was coming home from his Christmas dinner and he wanted to get some sleep.' I rebuffed him, and it worked. He insisted – just as I'd expected, just as I'd hoped. 'I'm Reda, couldn't we hang out? Maybe we could get a drink, or I could roll us a joint, or—' I tell him I don't do drugs. And then he doubles down, 'No problem, we'll just talk . . . What's your name?'

When I described this interaction to the police, I tried to tell it in chronological order, the way they wanted, but the male officer, the one sitting at the desk, kept interrupting; he'd never let me finish . . . 'But you're sure he had a handgun? You know that changes everything, right?' I looked to his colleague, asking her for help, I was begging her to help me. For the moment she kept her distance, and he went on: 'Still, rape is pretty bad, too – they say it can be worse than death.'

I listen.

'So then Reda says why don't they go up and have a drink at Édouard's place. He wasn't stupid, he knew he lived nearby. He must have known from the way he was walking. Guys like that, they know what they're doing. And since Édouard still wasn't saying yes or no, the other guy starts trying to take it back about the drugs.

'He says, I'll keep the hash in my pocket if you're not into that, I won't touch it, we don't have to smoke. He says they could just have a couple of beers together, that's all. Just a couple of beers. And he wouldn't stay long, either, and Édouard says he hates beer. And I'm thinking, This takes some serious patience. I wouldn't be wasting my time on some random guy who kept telling me no. And see, right there, it doesn't make sense. That he's patient. Why is he being so patient, right?'

I kept saying no and he kept walking along beside me, still smiling the whole time, still just as energetic and undiscouraged; maybe he'd noticed the hesitation in my voice, maybe he'd seen me glancing over, maybe he knew how little it would take to win me over, all I needed was the slightest gesture and he'd bring me round, I'd confess I'd wanted to talk to him ever since he stopped me on the square, all I'd wanted was to take him home with me, to put my hand on his, maybe he knew I was fighting, maybe he knew I was struggling, maybe he knew it was all I could do to hide how badly I wanted him. I remember how cold it was, and it was windy, too, so windy that my eyes were watering and I'd stopped even trying to dry them, and he was sniffling while he spoke, his words were punctuated with great burning sniffs and I could hear them echo through his nasal cavities. He turned away to wipe his nose on his hand, then he wiped his hand on his trousers, and it left a shiny trail. I didn't care. Ordinarily a thing like that would have made me sick. But not that night, not with him.

★

'But what I was trying to say is, the guy didn't seem suspicious. There was no reason for Édouard to be scared. It's not like he was trying to start some kind of fight. He was calm. He was friendly. But Édouard wanted to go home and he wouldn't budge. He just kept saying: I have to go home and read, I have to go home and read.

She takes another sip of water.

'So finally the guy asks the question. He puts out his hand and says what have you got there, and what does Édouard say? Books, they're just books, and Reda says to him, Interesting, and now I'm like, Édouard, have you never noticed that whenever you explain something to somebody, or tell somebody what you do, that's all they ever say, Interesting? Everything's "interesting", but if they're so interested how come there's never a follow-up question? Funny, right? What they mean is, they've heard enough. If you feel like going on about yourself, or telling them more about your life, well, that's up to you.

'And that's what I said to Édouard. I told him, You're not interesting. He didn't flinch when I said it. He just froze. I'm not saying this to put you down, I'm not try-ing to be mean, but when people tell you that what you do is "interesting", they're telling you a lie. If they say it to you, if they say it to me, if they say it to anyone, it's a lie. It doesn't make any difference who you are, you hear me, every life matters the same, and so why should the world take any special interest in yours? Don't kid your-self. People always think their own lives are so fascinating, and yes they realise everyone else thinks the same, but still they tell themselves that everyone else is wrong and they're right. But it doesn't work that way. I'm sorry to break it to you, but you can live in Paris or be a philoso-pher or whatever you want to do, it doesn't change a thing *(that part's made up, she never said that. I'm sure she thought it when we were talking, but she never said it).*

'We never get tired of lying to ourselves.'

Her husband doesn't speak any actual words. He just says 'unh-hunh' every now and then to show he's listen-ing, or when she asks him a direct question, and his grunts reach me through the door.

'I don't get it, I told him. Because really, come on, nobody believes these lies but still everybody tells them, even though they know better. And you, why pretend to be dumber than you already are? You must have known Reda was lying.

'It's exactly like with my neighbour Océane, when I'm at her house. Now, I admit she's plain, whatever – I say that not as a criticism, I love Océane – but the other thing is, and there's no way to get around it, she isn't thin. And it gets to her, poor thing. She feels it. She feels it because everybody rejects her, I mean the guys. They won't go near her. And since nobody's going to touch her, there she was, eighteen, nineteen years old, and still a virgin, everyone turned her down. You know how stupid they are, if you're walking by with Océane and there's a group of them hanging out at the bus stop, or wherever, and they're drinking they'll say, Here comes double-wide Océane, or, Here comes Océane, you can't pick her up but you can roll her, all that kind of thing. You know how bad they can be. Whatever, they're trash. As I've got older I've seen guys that, if you get them off on their own, they can be nice enough, but I don't care – as soon as you get a few of them together, that's it. Men turn into idiots when there's a few of them around. You don't even recognise them any more.

'So on Wednesday afternoons it's become our little tradition, we all get together at Océane's to play cards and we play double solitaire. Even if there's three of us, we play in teams. Or we play tarot. And every single time, we just know that sooner or later Océane is going to say it, she's going to say how bad she feels, and every time, sure enough, at a certain point she says it, and when she says how bad she feels, about herself, about her body – and you can be sure she'd never say that to any-one but us girls, because we support each other, because we stick together – what I say is: What do you mean, Océane? You're so pretty, don't you listen to those guys, you know how guys are, they've all got their head up their arse, that's just the way they are. And the funny thing is, as I'm saying it, I know I'm lying – not about guys being dumb, I'm lying about her body – and Océ-ane knows I'm lying, and it's like I feel this chill come over me because of what I think, not what I say, and Vanessa, who's usually there with us too, she'll chime in, she'll nod her head and say, It's true, you really are pretty, Océane, you've just got a beauty that's all your own, you can't go comparing yourself with the girls in the magazines, you know if you catch them when they wake up, before they do all their make-up and hair and everything, they're pigs – they only look good because they put on all of that foundation. But you're beautiful the way you are, naturally. That's what really matters, to have a natural beauty. And none of us believes a word we're saying. None of us, but we pretend to, and each of us leans on the other girl's lie, hoping her lie will make it all a little more true, and what I mean to say is, that must be how it was with Édouard, he had to know the guy was handing him a line *(but so what if Reda didn't care what I had to say, that truth meant nothing to me, the form meant everything, the content nothing; it was fine if Reda had no interest in the content of what I said, as long as he wanted to win me over, even if that meant telling a lie).*

'He asked some more questions, nothing special, just the questions people ask, How long have you lived in Paris? Are you doing anything later on? And Édouard was still thinking: I have to go to bed. I have to go to bed. But he told me it was like that sentence made less and less sense. It made less sense with every step they took. That's when the guy asked if Édouard's family came from England or from Germany, he says, I can't

49

figure out if you're English or German, and Édouard says, Unfortunately, neither one. He laughed and told him what our father liked to say about our family. He likes to say how our parents were French, and theirs were French, and theirs, and theirs, and theirs – that our bloodline is pure. And now the guy finds it funny, too, our father's saying. In fact it cracks him up.'

5

He told me that he was Kabyle and that his father had
come to France in the early sixties. This was twenty
years before Reda was born. When we met, Reda must
have been in his early thirties. They sent his father to a
designated immigrant hostel somewhere to the north of
Paris, I forget the exact town, with no more than a
change of clothes and a few things stuffed into a little
suitcase – and not because he had nothing, though it's
true he didn't have much, but because he wasn't allowed
to bring any more with him; as if it weren't enough to
be poor, he had to seem poor too. Reda began to tell me
all this when we were standing outside my building, but
it was later – when we were lying together in bed and I
was begging to know more about him, about his life –
that he told me the rest. He rested his head on my chest
as he talked. I just listened. I ran my fingers over his skin
and listened. His father had crossed all of Kabylia to get
away. He hiked day after day, all by himself. He didn't

want to go with the others. He crossed the desert, he slept on the sand and in the dirt, hidden in the bushes.

I told Clara his father must always have dreamed of leaving, of running away. It's an ordinary dream, but the truth is, ordinary dreams are often what set us free. Maybe, I told her, he wanted to go to a place where he had no friends, no family, no past; that's how I felt the first time I left for the city, and I can't be the only one, and of course I know it's naïve — I was naïve — but naïveté, I've learned, is a necessary condition of escape. Without naïveté you'd never try. Clara listened as I made my speculations, and chimed in with her own. By leaving, I said, he must have thought he could get rid of his past, that with no past, no history, and thus no shame, he could try on all the styles and poses we secretly want to try but deny ourselves, he could have followed every crazy urge we dream of but suppress, whether it's dyeing our hair, walking differently, laughing differently, getting a tattoo, whatever urge we silently dismiss for fear we'll be put in our place: 'Who do you think you are? What are you playing at? What is this part you're acting out? This isn't you, we don't know you any more.' Even if the change is superficial. How we speak, or dress, or hold ourselves. Reda said his father came here to make money, but that doesn't prove anything one way or another.

He left partly to redeem the past. When he thought of leaving, it wasn't just to help the son he would have, the son he already planned to have; it wasn't to improve his own situation – it was too late for him; he told himself, 'It's too late' – nor was he trying to reinvent the present, it was too late for that, too; no, when he took action, it was to reinvent the past. He wanted the 'after' to give meaning to the 'before', he dwelled on his son's future success – as if in the final moments of a fight to the death – so that he could see it as the result of his own life, so that he could reassure himself that everything he'd done, lived through, seen and endured had not been for nothing, as if he'd done it all for this one reason, as if it all had meaning – a meaning he'd intended, wished for, researched, weighed, as if none of it were a waste; as if all his past suffering and failure were investments in the future, sacrifices willingly made towards the future. The past is the one thing we can change, and I have no doubt he feared the future less than he feared the past.

When his father arrived, he was carrying a map that showed the way to the hostel. He had admired this map for weeks before he actually made the trip; it seemed to him that each letter might come to life and materialise before him, that each letter might live and breathe, that if he looked hard enough at the map, he might discover the truth – the masked and hidden truth, for now completely silent – about the new life he had in store. Now that he was actually here, he stopped, he nearly turned round and went back the way he'd come. Didier once said: 'When we get something we really want, from that moment on, our only thought is how to put it behind us.' There he was at the door of the hostel and he couldn't do it, he couldn't decide, he couldn't move, he thought: Now I have to ring the doorbell. But he didn't. Maybe it was raining, and maybe he was smiling; maybe a faint smile flickered over his features, wet with rain, and betrayed his happiness because we associate rain with gloom, and a smile in the rain stands out; a smile in the rain means that much more. I see him standing in front of the hostel. I see him pacing in front of the great big building, back and forth – a long scene of hesitation as he moves from one side of the picture to the other, while across the road the street sweepers laugh in their fluorescent overalls, doubled over with laughter to see him lost in his quandary.

And then Reda told me that, in his father's story, after all this hesitation, his father did it. He rang the bell. And the door swung slowly open. But no one appeared. The ray of light on the tiled floor grew wider and wider, it changed shape, the daylight stretched into the hallway and was swallowed up; and I see him from behind, Reda's father, I see the nape of his neck, as strong and beautiful as his son's, I can visualise the door opening so slowly that it's almost hard to bear. And then – no one. Nobody there. Only darkness. After peering into this darkness for a second or two, he started to wonder if anyone had opened the door at all, or whether it was just a gust of wind, the wind and nothing more, or whether in his nervousness he'd opened the door himself, by accident. But he didn't move. Certain people freeze when they're afraid. And in the doorway there loomed out of the darkness, ever more distinctly, the face of a man – the manager of the place – his features growing sharper and sharper, his nose hooked like a beak, his eyebrows bushy; he may have been slightly drunk, I don't know, Reda didn't say; maybe when he sees the man loom up and open his mouth to speak, Reda's father feels a warm breath of whisky on his face, or perhaps it wasn't that way at all – what's the difference? – maybe he never drinks, or as he would say: he never touches alcohol, maybe alcohol disgusts him and so do cigarettes, maybe he's always scrupulously clean, maybe he gives off an unvarying scent of Marseille soap and hair tonic, as stomach-turning as the stench of whisky breath. His father told him a lot about the manager of the hostel, but Reda told me very little except that he was a veteran; and later on I read up on the subject and discovered that most of the managers of these immigrant hostels were indeed veterans. They'd know how to maintain order, it was thought, and would understand the psychology of the immigrants, since some of them had seen action in the former colonies.

He told me, too, that the manager treated his father a little better than he treated the others, and much better than he treated the Arabs, because he was Kabyle, and the manager thought Kabyles were worthier, braver, and actually cleaner than Arabs – and no doubt his father shared this point of view; I know Reda did, and I suppose he picked that up from his father. I have no way of knowing. But that night when we were still on the street he mentioned not liking Arabs, I can't remember the exact slur, I can't remember what word he used, only the violence he carried inside him; I pretended I hadn't heard, of course I couldn't yet think what I thought a few days later – that ultimately Reda and the police spoke about Arabs the same way *(months later, when a friend pointed out that Reda was just as racist as the police, albeit for reasons of his own, it made me angry, it filled me with anger and contempt; I couldn't stand to hear Reda insulted, I wanted to protect Reda from this friend of mine; if someone had to speak ill of Reda, I wanted it to be me and me alone; only I was allowed – because Reda owed me).* That night I simply ignored anything that seemed bad about Reda, although I didn't realise that's what I was doing; only later did it strike me how much reality I set aside in order to keep what I liked.

When he said his father had always described the manager as a violent and tyrannical man, all of a sudden I saw him – and it was images of Ordive that flashed into my mind; when people are talking, I can't control the flow of memories, they simply come to me, they tunnel their way in, and they are my only access to the present; and so while I listened to Reda, I thought of Ordive, a woman I hadn't seen in ten years, fully convinced that this manager looked like her. She was elderly. She lived alone, she was one of those grim and solitary women one generally finds in small villages, routinely associated with the figure of the witch; we'd see her on the silent roads, and since it was the North, the roads were nearly always shrouded in a light mist; up and down she went, though we never knew where she was going, maybe nowhere, perched on a bright orange bicycle that was too big for her. She was universally reviled, on that point there was unanimity. Many stories and rumours were told about her and passed down across the years, so many stories, they seemed never to fade away, they were never forgotten, no matter how she tried to bury them in her silence. I think people found her silence artificial in some way – it wasn't that she never spoke, it was that she seemed to be keeping silent, which is a very different thing, and everyone in the village knew the stories weren't true, but everyone repeated them all the same. The ones who told the stories knew they weren't true and so did the ones who listened then turned round and spread them, but people told the stories anyway. And so the shared lie grew and swelled. It had been retold for so many years, I don't know whether everyone knew it as the fruit of a mass hallucination, or whether they ended up believing their own lie and forgetting where it came from.

Two stories were told more often than the rest; the

first was that she'd slept with Germans during the war, for money; I'd hear it over and over again: 'That one made a fortune running around with the Krauts.'

Second, they said she was partly to blame for the death of her granddaughter, who died of a terrible illness when she was still in nursery school. This was a subject that came up all the time, like a verbal tic; even if no one had any particular wish to bring it up, the story came up, again and again, during card games or summer games of pétanque on the red dirt of the village pitch, as automatically as conversations about the weather. The little girl said her head hurt, and Ordive's daughter, the mother of the child, went to the doctor, and the doctor said it wasn't serious, 'nothing to worry about', just migraines, 'it's normal at that age, the way they run around, especially nowadays,' and it didn't go away, the little girl would be crying with pain, she kept complaining about it at school, so Ordive's daughter went back to the doctor, and the doctor prescribed acetaminophen. She took it for eight or ten months. Then one day they found out it wasn't migraines, it was cancer. The news spread like a powder trail, each new person who *knew* told three others who told three others, and so on, and before the afternoon was over everyone had heard. The whole time the disease had been growing, and all she took was over-the-counter pills, and the bad cells had proliferated, it was too late, they couldn't do anything to treat her. The child lived only a month or two more. For those one or two months, the impending death was on everyone's lips, everyone had their own prediction of when it was coming, and this was always offered with a kind of false reluctance. And then one day it came.

For months people talked about the little coffin, the horror of that sight which had come much too soon, just as predicted, the white coffin on the church square, almost as tiny as a shoebox, and then no one dared to say anything bad about Ordive, they pitied her: 'Poor woman, she never deserved a thing like that,' they wept over her and for her, they gave her little gifts as a gesture of support, just to show her she wasn't alone – generally flowers and chocolates. Collections were taken up, some people decided to take up collections to cover the cost of the funeral; and their hatred found new outlets, as if it were a feeling that by its very nature could never disappear but only pass from one body to the next, leap from one group, one community, to the next; I told Didier, hate can exist without any particular individuals, all it needs is a place where it can come back to life. And then, as if it were irresistible, people expressed less and less pity for Ordive and her daughter, and soon, a month or two later at most, no one spoke of them at all, and then you began to hear people say that Ordive's daughter did have something to do with it after all; they said they hadn't realised at first but new information had come to light, time had done its work and now we knew the mother was to blame and so, indirectly, was the grandmother, Ordive; they weren't entirely innocent, they'd been careless, so people said; they hadn't taken the right precautions, they could have saved the child – everyone knew it wasn't true, everyone knew there was no evidence against them, but everyone went on with the proceedings; the ones who told the story knew it wasn't true and so did the ones who listened so they could spread it later on, but they told it all the same. And the collective lie grew and swelled.

Ordive was hated because of these rumours and because of her attitude: years of hatred and isolation had left her corroded with bitterness, and in that time her spite had grown – as we all know, people who are hated become hateful in the end. I was no different, I hated her too. She chased after children when she saw them in the street, she chased after me, and she would cry out, over and over: 'You have no manners, you should smile when you greet your elders, you should stop playing with that Game Boy or the computer all day long, you should get some fresh air, in my generation we knew how to amuse ourselves, they gave us three sticks and a piece of string and that would keep us busy till Monday,' and as much as I feel for her because of the persecution she endured, even though now I understand that her ordeal could only leave her full of resentment, that it could hardly be otherwise, at the time all I could do was hate her just as much as everyone else did; and when I imagined the manager of the hostel, hers was the name that came to my mind. Yesterday I told Clara – who was very familiar with Ordive – that it may have been cruel of me, but that giving her name to that man had seemed a kind of necessity.

As soon as Reda's father had spent an hour at the hostel, he knew all there was to know. He had met others who had been living there forever, he could tell from their knowledge of the place and how it worked and the schedule, and he could also tell – though Reda's father couldn't have said quite how – because they all looked, stood, talked, watched, laughed the same, apart from a detail here or there, they were like men produced by one single thing, born from the belly of one woman, one person, one creature: the hostel.

Within an hour he knew everything; he knew that for a few years he would have to sleep with four others in a tiny room – four men were given bunk beds, and the other one, the fifth, slept on a mat stretched out on the damp and mouldy linoleum floor. He understood that fires would be part of life in the hostel, that sometimes they'd be fatal – afterwards, if the fire had been hot enough, they would find charred bodies two or three times smaller than their actual height, shrivelled up in a puddle of solidified human fat, which dripped from the body when it burned. So I imagine. He knew that he could be deported for any reason, for 'bad behaviour', as the manager called it (without anyone knowing what 'bad behaviour' might actually mean), that he would be deported if he showed up late to the factory – of course his father's schedule was monitored, almost to the minute, Reda said; they told him no women, they couldn't have women in their rooms, or men from outside, friends from the factory for example, because the manager was afraid that without women, the men would make do with other men. His father must have realised that this power structure would force him to lie, he knew he'd have to lie to his family back home, to whom he sent money, he knew he would lie out of pride, and that when he went back he'd have to let them believe that his life in France was prosperous and basically pleasant, that all was well (and what is power if not this machine for creating lies, for forcing others to lie?).

Now and then the manager would invite Reda's father to visit him in his private apartment, when his wife and children were away. Reda's father would show up at nine on the dot, the manager would greet him at the door, glass in hand. He would offer him a seat. He would ask Reda's father if he minded a little music, and before he could answer, the manager would get up and turn on the radio. Reda's father hated this music. He found it obscene. But he said nothing. He didn't move, he sat frozen on the sofa each time this scene was repeated: for two hours the manager alone would talk, then would send him away when he got bored, saying, 'Some days I wonder what the fuck I'm doing here,' saying, 'Sometimes I want to get the fuck out and never see another brown face in my life,' saying, 'Sometimes I tell myself there has to be a country where you can do what you want and nobody fucks with you, no one tells you what's right or wrong, where you can walk around bare-arse naked and no one can say a thing – that's the country where I'm headed when I get out of here,' and Reda's father would sit there silent, stony-faced, disgusted by the music, disgusted by the man across from him.

But the worst part of his daily life wasn't the filth of the place or the authoritarianism of the manager, it wasn't the cramped rooms, though these were rarely more than five or six metres square, it wasn't the lack of any place to put your things, or the stench that spews from those toilets as if from the centre of the earth, through mouldy pipes and foul sewers, and which spreads everywhere in those buildings. It wasn't the insects, the cockroaches hidden in every crack, every fissure, under the rickety furniture, or the fires that punctuate life in the kitchens because of the faulty wiring. It wasn't even the sexual deprivation, or the resulting dreams, the obsession with women (or in some cases men), and the erections, hard and damp under the sheets, so hard they hurt when you wake up. What made life unbearable in the hostel, above all, was the noise. Everyone who's lived in one will swear to you, if you ask, that the absolute worst thing about a hostel is the noise. When they talk among themselves, that's what they talk about – the noise.

His father told him that, compared with the noise,

everything else seemed almost easy to deal with, because noise is one of the few things you can't get away from or do anything about. You can fix a wobbly bed, you can get hold of a new coffee maker, even if it's against the rules, you can find stuff for killing cockroaches, but what can you do about noise? You can't grab hold of it, if you went and slapped your neighbour because he slammed his door, what would it matter? The noise is everywhere, every hour of the day or night, and is practically autonomous compared with the people who are supposedly making it, the noise penetrates the body by way of the ear and reverberates in every cell, the noise troubles the silence of the inner organs. The tiny rooms where the immigrants slept, including Reda's father, had once been much bigger rooms, which were then subdivided, for lack of space, using thin boards and plywood. Some work the day shift, some the night. The incessant back and forth between work and the hostel, the creaking doors, the snores, the shouting in their sleep, the groaning beds, all their misery comes out in noise. It is impossible to rest; as the sleepless nights and restless sleep accumulate, fatigue makes them even more sensitive to the noise.

He was Kabyle. When I repeated this, and explained that his being Kabyle had profoundly affected the course of the evening, the officer – I can't remember whether it was the man or the woman – interrupted and said, 'So

Arabs are your thing?' They waited for me to answer, and I didn't say anything at first, then, in the idiotic way one does, I answered – as if the question had been a real question, as if it had been appropriate, as if it were acceptable – that he wasn't an Arab but a Kabyle, that I had studied that part of the world, and that thanks to my studies I was familiar with certain elements of Kabyle culture. I could even speak a few words. I've forgotten them now, but that night they were very present in my mind. I had told Reda that I knew a lot ('a lot' was an exaggeration) about Kabyle culture. He was amazed. But the police officer still looked sceptical, and he or she said: 'You're sure he was Kabyle? Obviously he could have been lying, and in fact the odds are—'; this time I stopped them, I said: 'When I spoke a few words to him in Kabyle, he recognised what I said.' He identified the words and translated them. I was concentrating, trying to get it right. My bad pronunciation amused him, he made fun of me. And I repeated this saying: *Azka d Azqa*. The coincidence, and his cynicism, seemed too overwhelming to be true, which is why I never mentioned the moment to Clara. Reda made me say it again. He said, 'This speaks of tomorrow, of the grave and of death.' I asked Reda to tell me about his mother. He said he'd tell me about her later on.

6

This whole time the grain of the door has filled my field of vision. I'm calm. I'm trying to stay calm. At this point, Clara tells her husband, I look Reda in the eyes and congratulate myself on having met him; I congratulated myself for having demurred when Geoffroy offered me another drink. Geoffroy had wanted to give me one last glass of wine before I went home, and I said no. I don't know why, but without thinking I pushed the bottle back when he passed it in my direction, I must have felt tired. After my night with Reda, I admitted to Clara, I wasted a lot of time on useless questions that led nowhere, dead-end questions, questions that had no answers — although they did manage to fill my days and keep me from doing anything besides asking them over and over again, while I limited myself to only the most mechanical tasks so I could keep my mind on the questions, for example making the bed even though I'd made the bed already several times that day, or finding something to pick up off the floor, a pen, a stray hair, or arranging the forks in the drawer; I wondered if what had happened with Reda would have happened if I'd said yes to that drink with Geoffroy and crossed the square five minutes later; I would become convinced that some little detail, something tiny and insignificant – if I'd had one more glass of wine, or if I'd stopped to tie my shoelaces a few metres away from the place de la République, or if I'd gone down a street I like better, because it's a nicer walk, because it's more picturesque, because it's more interesting – could have kept me from bumping into Reda, I would ask myself whether such a meaningless decision could have derailed the events of the night and the months that followed. I know in spite of everything that, even if it hadn't taken place that night, it would have happened sooner or later, in more or less the same way, that it was geographically inevitable.

We came to a brightly lit intersection, where the rue du Faubourg-du-Temple meets the quai de Valmy, and I slowed down, hoping we could talk just a little bit longer before I went home to bed. I'd barely met him, and still I was ready to beg him not to leave me; and I thought, *He's only interested in you because the streets are empty*; and I thought, *It's because there's nobody else around. It's because you're the only one still out on the street.*

We got near my house and Reda kept paying me compliments, some of which were strange and over the top, and the wind was still blowing, it went right through my clothes, my hair was sticking straight up. I tried to smooth it down, but as soon as I put my hand back into my jacket pocket – or even when I started to do so, as soon as my hand found the opening of the pocket or brushed the lining with my fingertips, up flew my hair.

That's when I realised I'd changed my mind. I was sure.

'He realised he'd go home with him. All of a sudden it just wasn't even a question. He was talking to Reda about his Arab background *(she's mistaken, he wasn't Arab)*, and that's when he realised that whatever part of him had been resisting wasn't there. It was dead. Anyway, that's how it felt – which makes it sound like they'd been walking for three whole days, but they were just right by his house, they'd gone, what, a few streets together *(less, actually, since I'd walked fifty metres alone between the time I returned the bike and the time Reda came up to me)*.

'So now it's a matter of time. Reda's getting impatient, he's had enough. He puts his finger on Édouard's mouth to make him stop talking *(and I felt the warmth of his finger on my lips, I felt it and I could even smell it)*, he said they couldn't just wander around all night, doing nothing, and frankly – look, you know what I think of the guy, but he had a point, frankly that's just how it is, you've got to make up your mind. He says they have to do something, they can't spend all night there on the street like a couple of bums. Édouard looks at him. He's not answering. He just quietly looks down. He doesn't know what to say, so now the guy insists, he says, What's up, are we going someplace or not?

'But I'm making him sound pissed off – and he wasn't. He wasn't at all pissed off the way he said it. Impatient, maybe, but I don't know how to put it – he wasn't angry impatient, he was impatient like someone who can't wait to get what he wants, and who knows it's going to happen, and wants it to happen. You see what I mean. He was happy impatient.

'He works up his nerve and then he just comes out and says it, mid-sentence. Do you want to have sex with me? Just like that. In those very words, I swear. Well! Obviously that's exactly what Édouard had been wanting to hear. Might as well ask a dog if he wants a bone. For a while now, it's what he'd been waiting for. He'd been wanting Reda to go faster, to pick up the pace. That's the only reason he'd been resisting – not to shut him down, but so he'd come out with it.

'But it was too violent. The way he asked the question was so blunt, it was like Édouard's body reacted all on its own, like if you take a little hammer and tap your knee. Not him, but his body. Like his body couldn't catch up to his head – but I don't really know how to say this either, because in his head he'd already made up his mind. He was sure. It was all sorted out in his head, everything was settled. He knew what he wanted, and what he wanted was to get Reda back to his place. To get Reda into bed. I'll spare you the details, but let's just say there wouldn't be any more reading that night. Books, what books?

'His head was saying yes, but his body told him no. To the point that he was actually surprised to hear himself say no – I'm only telling you what he told me, how he heard his body arguing against him, how his head wanted to go upstairs but his body lied to Reda, as if by instinct, and his head insulted his body *(and I hated my body)* but it didn't do any good, his body kept on lying and he said *(or rather, it was my body talking)*, You have no idea what a bad scene it would be if I took you home, not with my family there, oh my god if my family found me with a guy I can't even think, it'd be the end. I swear, you'd never get out in one piece. My brother would kill me, too, he's always saying how he won't put up with that under his roof. To him it's the worst. It would mean total war. They'd kick me out and they'd hurt you, they'd really mess you up.

'And frankly? I'm thinking, Thanks a lot. Couldn't he have found some other lie? Couldn't he have found a lie that didn't turn us into a bunch of bigots? There's a whole lot of lies out there to choose from. I'm just saying, he could have come up with something else. We've always respected him for what he was, always, and when he told us he was different – that very day he told us, I remember like it was yesterday – what did we tell him? We told him it didn't change a thing, we'd love him just the same *(she's lying)*, no matter what, and for us he'd still be the same person. We told him all that mattered was his happiness, all we cared about was he was happy *(she's lying)*, we told him we're family and that's what counts. My mother told him, All I want is for my children to be happy and to live good happy lives, that's all I ask, I don't care about money, money doesn't matter, all I ask is happiness for my children. Just happiness. And that was that. Of course we asked him not to make a big deal of it in the village when he came back, not that he did come back very often, but the once in a blue moon when he did, because then we'd be the ones who had to deal with it when he left. We were the ones who'd have to pay. And how would that have gone down? You know how the people here are, you know them as well as I do, they're country people, we'd never have heard the end of it, not for the next five generations – you know it's true. You think they'd let us live down a thing like that? Come off it. Think of all the remarks we'd get, and what a life that would be, with some kind of nasty remark every day, and the constant little digs. That's not even counting what they'd say behind our backs, but that, too – and him with his little brother and sister still in school, they'd have been picked on, their lives would have been ruined. Because the people around here, they're country people. You breathe in nothing but cow shit and pollen all your life, studies show, you're going to end up retarded. But what can I do about it? I didn't make them that way. So we asked him not to mince around too much and not to go around in girly clothes, is that so much to ask? The only person we made him promise not to tell was his grandfather, and not because his grandfather wouldn't have understood, but because it might have killed him – and it's not like *he* did anything wrong, is it? You can see what I mean. He's from another generation, you can't judge different generations by one single standard, he had a hard life, first working on the farm, then fighting in Algeria, then working at the factory, and on and on and on. He just wouldn't get it. He wouldn't be capable of understanding, and honestly why should we throw this at him now, on top of all the other shit old people have to deal with?

'But we accepted him as he was *(not true)*. And that's what makes me wonder. That's why the whole thing always leaves me a little uneasy. Sometimes I think Édouard told us he was different not so we could be closer to him or know him better – because deep down, you tell me if I'm wrong, that's why you tell somebody a secret: to bring them close – but actually for the opposite reason. In his heart he didn't want us to accept him. He hoped it would make us push him away, because we'd be hurt and angry that he'd been keeping this secret of his, and we'd reject him, and then afterwards he could go and tell everybody, in that stuck-up way he has, You see? It's their fault I'm too cowardly to have a relationship with my family. That way he could avoid all the responsibility and still tell everyone, with a clear conscience, They're the ones who threw me out, I didn't abandon them, it's all their fault. You know how these things work. What I think, when I have time to think about it — and I've never said anything to my mother, I've kept it to myself, because why hurt her? — is that once he saw we accepted him, secrets and all, it made him hate us. He hated us because it ruined his plans, because he couldn't go and tell everyone how everything was our fault, and sometimes I think he never forgave us for accepting him how he is. That's if you ask me. But now, what was I saying? Oh right, Édouard. So he apologises for not asking the guy up. He says, I'm sorry, I can't take you home — he hears himself apologising or, how he puts it, he hears his body apologising, not his head — sometimes he doesn't make a hell of a lot of sense, but whatever, you get the idea. He hears himself apologise and then Reda, what does he do? He takes his hand, again, a second time, in the middle of what he's saying. He grabs Édouard's hand and he presses it against his dick, so Édouard can feel it through his sweatpants. He was wearing sweatpants. That took Édouard completely by surprise. I don't mean the sweatpants, of course. I mean what he did with his hand, and then the guy says: Just let me buy you a drink down here, at the café, or we'll get a cup of coffee, for five minutes, just give me a chance, give me a chance, give me a chance, and he says, My treat. Please? This whole time Édouard wasn't saying anything, and so he takes his hand again and pulls it against his crotch and says all this stuff like, You're so beautiful, you're the most beautiful blond I've ever seen. You have the bluest eyes. And so Édouard sighs. He invites the guy upstairs.'

Now that I'd lied and then suddenly changed my story and admitted that I didn't live with my parents, Reda wanted to know why, when I was barely twenty years old, I didn't live at home and most of all why I hadn't gone home for Christmas. Was it because of my studies? I explained that becoming a postgraduate student was actually a result of my having escaped from my family. The escape came first. The idea of further study had only occurred to me later, when I realised that was pretty much the only way I could get away from my past, not just geographically, but symbolically, socially – that is, completely. I could have gone to work in a factory like my brother, three hundred kilometres from my parents, and never seen them again; that would have been a partial escape. My uncles, my brothers would still have lived inside me: I'd have had their vocabulary, their expressions, I'd have eaten the same things, worn the same clothes, I'd have had the same interests, I'd live more or less the way they did. Studying was the only real escape route I could find. Reda asked me: 'But still, you go see them all the time, right? They come visit you? You must see them – they brought you up, after all.' I took this as a sign of his generosity.

★

'So they went up to Édouard's. They ran up the stairs. Not for any reason, just one of them took off running and the other followed. Like kids. They were laughing and cheating, trying to hold each other back by grabbing each other's clothes *(our laughter echoed in the stairwell)*. He told me they were laughing and panting and sweaty and when he got to the door – it's five floors up – he wanted to open the door but he couldn't find his keys. For a change. And then? He panicked. He was afraid he'd ruined everything; suddenly their whole conversation, even the fact they'd met, had all been a waste of time because he'd locked himself out of the apartment. I told him, I don't see why it would have been such a waste of time, you could have seen each other the next day, and he answered back – I could tell he didn't like my interrupting – all right, maybe not a literal waste of time. At any rate, I found the keys.'

I didn't find the keys by myself. Reda actually slipped his hands into my pockets and rummaged through them one by one. He let me feel the heat of his hands through the fabric of each pocket, and my cock grew harder and harder, feeling his fingers so close. His fingers were warm and moist. He found the keys himself. That detail is just one of many things I never shared with my sister or the police, only with Didier and Geoffroy. For example, even though this moment was woven deeply into the fabric of the night, and into my feelings – in the most general sense of the word – towards Reda, I never told the police how I turned out the lights, and how the inky blue light from outside sifted through the cracks in the blinds, and how I saw that blue light shining down in thin stripes over Reda, over his chest, his back, his face. I didn't tell them that Reda offered to give me a massage before he ran away, long before, before the rape, before the scarf, before the anger, and that I said yes and stretched out on my stomach. He told me to relax, to breathe as deeply as I could, to hold the oxygen in my lungs then let it out slowly, in long, deep exhalations; and he whispered, 'Think of something beautiful,' and I answered, 'You,' and he laughed and he told me, 'All right, think of a beautiful place,' and I answered, 'You.' If I'd told that to anyone but Didier or Geoffroy I would have felt ridiculous.

With the police I simply told them we went inside the apartment. I left it at that. Opposite me, the two officers were so static they might have been part of the décor, just like the chairs, or the yellowed anti-drug posters on the walls. I already grasped the importance of their listening. This week, while I've been talking to Clara – or whenever I've talked to Didier and Geoffroy, ever since the day after I filed the report – I've noted all the inappropriate and racist remarks the police made, I've noted their complete inability to understand my behaviour, I've noted their obsessions, I've explained everything that separated them from me, everything that made me hate them; at the same time, they helped me in a crucial, decisive way, they represented a place where it was possible for me to say what I had to say, and where this was sayable. From the moment I walked in, they made me feel clearly authorised to speak, and from then on my words would bear the trace of this possibility, which existed in my mouth thanks to them.

The one sitting at his desk stopped me when I described how we went in. 'At this point he had shown no signs of aggression?' I answered: 'None. On the contrary, he was funny. Solicitous. Strangely solicitous, now that I think about it, considering we'd just met.' And the policeman: 'You gave him a drink? Would you say he had been drinking before you met?'

He mentioned having had something to drink, but he wasn't drunk. He was in full control of his movements. He didn't smell of alcohol. He slipped off his shoes, staring the whole time at the piles of books on my floor. I looked at him. We had turned the light back on (was it so we could get undressed?). He tilted his head so he could read the titles on the spines, he read them aloud under his breath, he turned towards me. Did I have anything to drink? I had nothing in the house. But then I remembered – I did have a bottle of vodka in the freezer, a Polish friend had given it to me when he came to Paris, and since I don't care for vodka, the bottle hadn't been touched, it was full. I poured some into a tall glass, he took a sip or two. That was all he drank; I came up to him and we kissed. His breath smelled strongly of alcohol, even after just one sip. I sat down and opened my fly, my head back, eyes closed. He put down the glass and knelt in front of me.

The police wanted to know if I felt his gun when we kissed; if so, I didn't notice. In any case, he took off his clothes very quickly, and if I had felt something in the inner pocket of his jacket, I wouldn't have thought it was a gun. We made love a first time. We did it again four, five times, and in between times he slept next to me, he took little naps of a few minutes each, during which he clung to my arms, to my hair, he'd run his hand through my hair and grab hold of it as if he were afraid I'd run away. He put his legs between mine, and he covered my cock with his hand, or he'd hold it, he'd squeeze it in his hand. We'd wake up, sometimes we'd talk. Then we'd start again.

He got up three or four times during the night to go to the bathroom and rinse himself off. He would press himself against the sink, standing on tiptoe, slightly arched over the basin. He rubbed his cock with his hands, the muscles rippling in his back. He'd make the water run over his cock and his lower belly, which he rubbed in a brisk circular motion, and on his way back to bed he'd stop in front of the books. He picked up one thick volume and said, 'I never read, my parents wished I was good at school, but it wasn't my thing, I was always clowning around.' It's one of the sentences around which I tried, later, to imagine Reda's life, to construct meaning and explanations where there was only silence. I told Didier and Geoffroy that there would have been a day when Reda stood up from his chair. Slowly. This would have been in primary school. He'd been sitting down like everybody else and suddenly up he stood. He moves away from the chair, much too gracefully – if he'd stood up in a hurry, or roughly, or if he'd cried out, it would have actually been less unsettling to the teacher, much less unsettling; it would have been reassuring compared with this calm and controlled movement, too calm, too controlled, like nothing she was used to, like nothing she had the words to name. She didn't say a word. All the kids were watching Reda. I imagine a classroom awash with light. I imagine the sunbeams on the polished blond wood of the desks and on the yellow linoleum, which in the heat of the light from outside gives off a plastic smell. They've been writing. Everyone was quiet when Reda stood and walked over towards one of the windows. Over to the window he goes, he passes between the open backpacks lying scattered on the floor. He moves along the perimeter of the class-room, and the heads turn one after another to watch him, no one understands, the other students follow him with their eyes; and he moves gently on, still perfectly calm, and heads for the window and opens it just as gen-tly, as if all he wanted was to get some air, and that may be exactly what the others are thinking at first, 'He's going to open the window to get some air.' He opens the sash and swings one leg out of the window. It was my cousin Sylvain who did this. It was one of his exploits, people told the story in our family and at my school, the same school he attended ten years before me, where this scene took place. No one had forgotten, over the years the scene had become a constitutive myth of masculinity, a sort of ideal, an origin story of masculinity, a reference point against which boys would have to invent themselves; it was something they dreamed about, a fantasy they had to attain or at least strive for in any situation. It wouldn't be my cousin, in this version, but Reda. I'm transposing. He opens the window with his fingertips, and not one word breaks the astonished silence. Then his leg, in a sort of slow motion, lifts itself from the floor, bends, straightens, then bends a second time to pass over the windowsill. Then comes the explosion. At the same time that the teacher, who had been sitting there as silent and astonished as everyone else, realises what's going on and cries out, Reda cries out too – that's what my cousin did, according to the story I heard and repeated, in turn, many times – and it's a shout even louder and deeper than hers and it drowns hers out, it sounds puny, feeble, like nothing next to his, 'I'm going to do it, I'm fucking going to jump,' and the teacher panics, 'as you can imagine', I say to Didier and Geoffroy, it's like a tableau with the teacher on the right – hands clasped before her mouth, as well they might be, eyes wide, the only possible response a body can make at a moment of such complete impotence – and Reda on the left, the two of them almost perfectly symmetrical, Reda with his leg out of the window, yelling, 'I'm fucking going to jump, I'm going to throw myself out of this window,' his face bathed in the yellow light, eyes shining, the thick veins of his face swollen from shouting, especially on his forehead, spit shining on his lips; and the light is too yellow, everything around him is too yellow, including his spit, and he has to keep from laughing at his own performance because he exults in the attention, the fearful and admiring attention of the other kids, who at the same time know he won't jump, who hope he won't do it and also hope he will, who want him to jump. There wasn't any reason for him to do it. And that was the point of the story, I told Didier and Geoffroy, he did it for no reason. He didn't have anything against the teacher in particular, he just wanted to see her transformed, deformed, transfigured by panic, he wanted to make the other kids laugh, he wanted to show who he was, to embody absolute freedom – Reda or Sylvain, it doesn't matter which – he wanted to be the image of freedom at its most spectacular. It wasn't a matter of responding to some kind of conflict. He would create the conflict himself, he would produce it, he would invent it – he would be the one in control of time, so the others would have to respond, he would decide *when* the conflict must occur, and how much weight to give it, and everyone else would take their lead from him.

7

I no longer recognised what I was saying. I no longer recognised my own memories, when I spoke them out loud; the questions I was being asked by the police made me describe my night with Reda differently than I'd have chosen, and in the form that they imposed on my account, I no longer recognised the outlines of my own experience, I was lost, I knew that once I went forward with the story, according to their cues and directions, I couldn't take it back, and I'd have lost what I wanted to say; I felt that once the right moment to say something passes, it disappears for good and can never be retrieved, the truth slips away and out of reach; I felt that whenever I spoke a word in front of the police, other words became impossible, now and forever; I understood that there were certain scenes, certain things, I must never discuss if I wanted to remember all that had actually happened; I understood that the only way to remember was to forget, and that if the police forced me to talk about those things, it would mean forgetting everything.

Reda had spent two hours at my apartment.

'They were lying under the covers, they were talking, and Édouard kept asking questions and the guy kept saying: Later. I'll tell you later. I can't understand why Édouard didn't start to suspect that something wasn't right. The guy was acting weird.'

And then she says yes, in the end she does know why I didn't suspect anything, it's because I latch on to people too quickly, I can latch on to anyone, it's been that way since I was little, and I haven't changed; but she wouldn't say this to my face, she wouldn't express this idea in front of me, because she knows I'd say I behaved that way, and still do, because of how alone I was, because I was always rejected by our family, and she says she doesn't want to hear that. Because it isn't true.

'So then Reda says he has to go. He was some kind of off-the-books plumber. He had to start early the next day. You know the kind of thing, little jobs here and there, plumbing or wiring or fixing engines, same as the guys do here *(like those friends of your father's who'd do little repairs in somebody's backyard and then split the bottle they got as a thank-you present, their hands black with the grease from the power tools or the engines they'd been working on, grease that took days to wash off completely, or else the hard skin of*

their fingers would be covered in little white cracks, like tiny
blisters, because of the paraffin they used to get rid of the grease).

'He said he had to go – and even if we'll never really
know the truth, I'm pretty sure that he had it all mapped
out in his head. All the stuff he did later on. All of it. He
wasn't really about to leave, he was buying time and getting ready for what came next *(I don't believe it. Or maybe*
he planned to steal something, yes, he must have planned that
part, but really I don't think Reda had any idea what would
happen over the next few hours, over the rest of the night, not
that this makes it any less violent or evil, but I think the whole
thing happened in a stumbling, accidental, hesitating way,
without any premeditation; I think he behaved the way a person
does who's trying to adapt to his immediate surroundings, from
moment to moment; I think one improvisation led to the next,
and that he was – I won't say as bewildered as I was, but that
he, too, had lost his way, that he was at a loss. Once the situ-
ation changed, there was something improvisatory about his
manner – I was there; I saw it – something that gave the entire
scene an air of slapstick; there was even something funny –
though of course I see this only in retrospect, when I look
back – about his look of bewilderment; he kept looking embar-
rassed when he realised whatever it was he'd just done, it was as
if he kept falling into a trap of his own making, as if he were
helplessly carried along by a series of present-tense moments. I
think each decision made that night, by me or by him, instantly
made other decisions impossible, that each choice destroyed other
possible choices, and that with every choice he made he became

less free, just like me in my interview with the police). (Clara remarked the other day that none of these theories hold – he had a gun.)

'He asked Reda if he wanted to take a shower. He'd tried to ask for his number, but Reda wouldn't give it to him, he said no – and that right there, if you ask me, that shows he had the whole thing planned all along, Édouard disagrees but he's wrong. He's wrong. This wasn't his first time, he knew what to do and what to avoid and that's why he didn't get in the shower with Édouard. No way was he about to do anything that might trip him up later on – things you or I would do without thinking, because when you don't have a plan in mind, you don't think, you just do what you do and time flies by, but he was counting the seconds. He was doing the maths.'

I asked for his number, I promised I wouldn't bother him; but that seemed to irritate him somehow, and he looked away. I thought he must have a good reason, I assumed there must already be someone in his life, a man or a woman, and that he must be afraid they'd see a text from me if someday he left his phone lying around on a bureau or a table. Clara says I'll do anything to believe he wanted to give me his number, that for some reason it wasn't up to him. Yesterday she said I'm fooling myself, telling myself he was somehow acting against his will – when his will was exactly the problem. No doubt she's right.

He told me we could see each other again at this one

café, he was always there; it was an old Parisian café where he liked to go and play table football with his friends. He told me the name of the café. I never went to see whether it existed, but I did repeat the information to the police, and I've regretted it ever since.

Clara tells her husband that I walked over to my desk, I took a piece of paper that I'd torn out of a notebook, and I wrote down the name and address of the café where I went to write almost every day I lived in Paris, the same café where, a month before, I'd finished my first novel, *The End of Eddy*. He told me he'd come; I've never been back there again.

Reda got up and took a shower. We didn't shower together, we took turns. I watched him bathing through the steamed partition. I could make out the contours of his body, shifting with the motion of his hands as he lathered himself – but only just, because the shapes were blurred by the steam and drops of water on the plexiglas. I wished I could be his hands.

'So it turned out he wasn't in such a big rush after all. He showered and then he let Édouard take a shower. He gave him time to get out, and dry himself off, and put on underpants and turn on the light and say goodbye. It's strange, he could have just slipped out while Édouard was in the shower, but he didn't leave. He stuck around and he waited to say goodbye. He waited for Édouard to get dressed, and dry off, and turn on the light. And all that time he could have left. I mean, please . . . So don't let anyone try to tell me he was just . . . I'm sorry. Anyway, Édouard got out of the shower and he went to check the time on his phone. It's a thing with him. Ever since he got here, every five minutes he has to check the time on his phone. Otherwise he says he loses his bearings, he says he literally can't lift a finger, it's like he doesn't know where he is, like he's lost in time, like he's paralysed, for Christ sake, and when he talks that way I want to tell him, Why does everything have to be a drama? Lost in time, my arse. That kid and his notions. God only knows the things I've heard. But I was nice about it, the way I try to be. And so that's why he looked in his pocket, to check the time. But the phone was gone. The phone wasn't in his pocket – and Reda hadn't left after all, he was still there in the apartment and he was standing absolutely still. He was standing right beside him, not moving.'

8

On some level I knew why my mobile phone had disappeared, but I didn't dare say it, much less think it; in fact, I was doing all I could to avoid that thought.

Clara describes to her husband how, for no conceivable reason – since the phone obviously wasn't there – I kept feeling around in the empty pocket, as if I might suddenly make the phone reappear through sheer willpower and the movements of my fingers.

The next day, when I came to this part of the story, the female officer said: 'Yeah, here at the station . . . most of the robberies we see . . . they're usually committed by foreigners, by Arabs.' I didn't say anything, I didn't insult her because I didn't want to spend any more time there than I had to, and because I knew she was trying to bait me. I was looking for my phone, which I'd turned on before I got into the shower so I could check the time. I told the police, 'I thought it must be the wine I'd had before. Or that I must just be tired and that's why I couldn't find my phone.' I hadn't actually thought it was the wine, or my fatigue. I'd wanted to think those things, but deep down I had my own idea – I hated it but there it was, rooted in a deeper place. My mind generally knows which of my thoughts are true and which ones I've made up to please or flatter myself. Even when I pretend otherwise. And I thought: *You must have put the phone down without thinking. You must have dropped it on the pile of laundry by the sink.* I remember telling myself I could find my phone in the morning, but I didn't believe that, either.

Reda was still standing there, a few steps away. I went to kiss him one last time and when I put my hands on his jacket (why did I put my hands on his jacket?), which was warm because he'd left it next to the radiator, I felt something hard and rectangular. I saw, sticking out of his jacket, the grey and shiny corner of my iPad. I hadn't noticed it was missing. I looked over at the table where it was supposed to be. It wasn't there.

'His first reaction was, It made sense he should steal something. Reda, I mean. Which, please. That was a little too much. I said, Exactly how would it "make sense"? Because really, that pissed me off. I said, You lost me there, because frankly I don't see how it "makes sense" to go ripping somebody off. Maybe I'm just stupid, but I just don't see it. I don't. No matter how I rack my brains. They disgust me, thieves *(it's another of her obsessions, she grew up in a family where someone or other was*

always being accused of some wrongdoing, and it's still that way
today, because various cousins and even our older brother are
always getting in trouble with the law, and in reaction she
developed a sort of anxious code of honesty and a tendency to
judge, as if to distance herself from these realities, because they
were too close).

'And he told me: Maybe it wasn't fair. I'm not saying
it was fair. No, he told me, I'm only saying it made sense,
if he was actually going around doing odd jobs under
the table, trying to scrape together a few euros as a
handyman, and if he was struggling and had to ask
people he knew, if he had to ask his friends, to give him
work? Having to be pushy like that? Having to humili-
ate himself? Because it is humiliating, you know it is:
Isn't there anything you need done around the house, or,
If you hear of anyone who needs a painter . . . So when
Édouard saw that Reda had stolen from him, he thought,
in his shoes he'd do the same. He wouldn't have acted
any better. He thought it would have made less sense if
Reda *hadn't* stolen from him.

'I never told on him to our parents, because I knew
he'd get a beating. They'd have beaten the shit out of
him and I have to say, they'd have been right. But I know
when he was younger, Édouard stole things, too. He
started stealing because he needed the money *(of course her*
code of honesty breaks down when it comes to family).

'I used to see him do it. He didn't know I was watching, but I saw him. He'd go out with his friends, the ones

from the bus stop. They'd go out, five or six of them in the one little car. In the middle of the night. No problem, one would just have to sit on somebody's lap. So they'd pack themselves in and they'd open the windows because six kids in one car, maybe you've never tried it, but it's no picnic, with them steaming everything up and their BO, and no one can breathe, it's like sitting inside a tin can. You can't even see through the windscreen. I mean, please.

'Everyone would have a hammer. Édouard would take our father's red hammer from the toolshed. I'd already noticed when he started going out to the toolshed with his backpack, since frankly the toolshed had never been his favourite place to go. He spent more time in the bathroom, if you know what I mean. But one night after the news came on and we were doing the dishes I realised he'd gone out to the toolshed, even though he never missed the news. And then I thought: Who takes a backpack into a toolshed? Then and there I knew something was up, I could tell he had something to hide. I've got a nose for that kind of thing.

'One day I secretly watched him. I hid behind the curtain and I waited for him to come out of the toolshed. I thought: You'll see, you'll just see. You're going to find out what happens when you get up to stupid shit. You'll see. And you better believe I was hidden behind that curtain. I was peeking through the fabric without touching so he couldn't see. I'd thought of everything. When you see a curtain move that's it, game over, especially those curtains we had. I was even breathing softly, to make sure the curtain wouldn't blow around. To keep it from trembling. And so then I went out to the toolshed. I'd already checked it out the day before, so I knew exactly what there was and where everything was kept, where it sat on the table or hung on the walls. I'd set my trap. That's how I figured out he was taking the hammer, and I started my little investigation and soon I had him bang to rights.

'Now our father would have lost his mind. He'd have gone apeshit – you don't steal a man's hammer. A man's hammer is sacred. But really, at the end of the day, even though he'd have been furious, because he always said how stealing was the worst, how it was for hoodlums and bums, and how he'd never put up with stealing in his house, I just know he couldn't have helped seeing it as good news. Secretly. Not that he'd have said so, he was a father after all, he had his pride and couldn't have come out and said it, but he'd have been relieved because for him stealing a hammer would have turned Édouard into a man. It would have meant he was tough. And even if he'd screamed and shouted and given Édouard the beating of his life – and there really would have been hell to pay – I just know it would have made him smile, sort of, when he found out and even afterwards, when he was giving him the belt, because he would have been able to say: Now that he's stolen, now that he's disobeyed his father, Édouard has finally become a man. He's taken action. He's done something dangerous, like a man. At long last. He'd have thought both things at once, and why not? Say what you like, I'm sure it would have made him sort of smile. But we'll never know, because I never told, so there was no beating and no smile. What can you do.

'I kept my mouth shut because I wanted to protect him. I didn't want him to get into trouble. Even if in my own mind it was wrong what he was doing, I'm not like that, I never was a telltale. He was still a baby so I thought, Give it time, it's just an urge, like having to pee, so let him piss it out of his system. He must have been fourteen or fifteen, the others about the same, one or two years older at the most. Only Brian was older, he was the one with the car because he was old enough to drive. He had a car of his own. He'd pick up the other boys and they'd go tearing off like a bunch of lunatics to some dump. They could have had an accident, they could have killed somebody, driving that way at night, but they were too selfish to think of other people, they just had to go tearing around. You could see them coming a mile away, if you wanted to. All you had to do was look, because they were pretty much the only ones on the road at that time of night, with everyone asleep. When I knew what they were up to, I'd look down from my bedroom window and watch the car driving away, windows open, towards old man Bailleul's cornfields. I'd see the headlights get smaller and smaller until they disappeared in the woods, and the sound got invisible too.

'So off they'd go. They'd wear dark colours and when they got to the dump they'd hop over the fence. They'd give each other a leg up, so I learned, and they'd bring bolt cutters for the padlock, but their only light was the moon. Just the moon. When they came home they'd have such filthy clothes. He was a bad driver, Brian, because he got his licence in the army and an army licence is meaningless, all you need is a pulse. And what would have happened if one of them had fallen, trying to get over the fence, what if one of them got impaled on a spike like some of those fences have? It happens all the time, just read the paper. Exactly how smart would they have looked then? People do die for some very stupid reasons.

'It all came out in the end, the way these things do. So I also know Brian would always check to make sure there wasn't a surveillance camera or a guard or, most of all, a dog. Dogs would have been the worst. They didn't use torches, only the moon. In fact they waited for nights when the moon was full *(I have no idea how she knows so much about it)*. And once they got into the dump they'd take pretty much anything they could find – washing machines, appliances. They'd lift them up together and carry them out to the boot and then they'd get out as fast as they came. I wish I'd been there to move them along – What are you, slow? Get a move on! I'd have loved to see their faces, but you know how I am. They stashed it all in this big open shed behind Brian's house, on the edge of a field. The next day – Édouard was always staying over at Brian's, on a camp bed in the living room – the next day they'd take their hammers and break down whatever they'd brought back. Then they'd sell it for scrap to a guy down the road. What they were really after was the copper they use in some appliances, that's where the money is. A coil of copper wire costs real money.

'It would have been so easy for them to get caught. The whole thing could have ended badly, frankly I don't know why it didn't, it's a miracle, especially with the noise they made, taking a dead washing machine apart with a bunch of hammers. Try taking a hammer and hitting the drum of a washer-dryer, you'll get the idea. You could hear it up and down the street. The neighbours couldn't work out what was going on, they found it unusual. That's what they told me once I'd launched my little investigation, and so to cover for them I said: Oh, it's nothing, just a project for school, you know how school is nowadays – they make them do all kinds of crazy things. They can't even read or count and here the teachers have them monkeying around with a bunch of microscopes and god knows what else like a bunch of Zulus.

'But Édouard didn't do it as much as the others. Partly because he was scared and partly because they'd already got into trouble once before over this other thing, this burglary they'd set up; they'd all planned the whole thing together, the same gang – oh, and that's what they called themselves, the Gang. Édouard used to leave the house before we'd finished eating and he'd say: I'm going to meet up with the Gang at the bus stop, and I'd be thinking, the Gang, the Gang my arse, if you think anyone's impressed by five hicks on rusty scooters covered in cow shit or some falling-apart old boat you bought off your cousin in the next village, and he felt sorry for taking your money, you're even stupider than you look. This isn't Chicago. No one's impressed. And then one day they went too far.

'They broke into the house of one of the village girls, they broke into her house and they ripped her off. They took advantage of the fact that this girl had fallen in love with one of the guys in the Gang. She'd been in love with him a long time. It wasn't love any more, it had actually driven her crazy, it was obsession, but the thing was she could never go up and talk to him because he was always hanging out with the guys and was never by himself and they would have made fun of her if she had come up and tried to talk to him while they were all together. They'd have gone on about lovebird this and lovebird that, Lovebird incoming. Lovebird at five o'clock. The expressions they used. They couldn't even talk like normal people. So apparently nothing had happened between them, but all the same she was in love.

'So that's when they came up with their retarded idea.

'Check this out. They said to the one she was in love with: Here's what you do, you go over to Constance's place and make her think you want to do the nasty, then you take her up to her bedroom. She'll totally go for it, all you have to do is ask, she's begging for you to pop her cherry, haven't you seen the way she's been staring at you all year? She's not exactly subtle. And meanwhile, while you're up there, we'll slip in the front door, so be sure she leaves it unlocked, and then we'll just walk out with whatever we can carry. And then we'll divvy it up.

'The girl, Constance, fell for it. The poor thing was in love. It was a piece of cake. So that night they let themselves into her house and it was all they could do not to burst out laughing, because to them it was all really funny. They filled up their backpacks and what do you think they took? Did they take the jewellery, the valuables? No, you overestimate their intelligence – always a mistake. What they took was her DVD player and her PlayStation and the games that went with it, and they put those into their backpacks and they left without making any noise, without banging the door, while Constance was fooling around with the boy upstairs. They took off running. They went to Steven's backyard, Édouard told me – he never told me about the scrap metal but he did tell me this – and they made a circle and danced around the stuff they'd stolen, can you imagine, they were singing and hugging each other and they were such idiots they were proud of themselves, like it was the heist of the century and they were a bunch of crime lords, like now they were men. So they partied all night long. They popped some beers and complimented each other on having stolen – not even some jewellery or a girl's bike, as I've said, no, but some Pokémon PlayStation or Harry Potter, or whatever the hell it was, and that's the thing: They were leaping around over a game they would never even play, except in their case they were so stupid and immature that they actually did play those games, they'd spend all day in front of the TV doing exactly that. Like the morons they were. But then to their surprise the girl worked everything out – so the question was how on earth could she have guessed? They suspected the boy of having spilled the beans because, according to their theory, he'd actually fallen in love with her, even if he wanted to play the bad boy in front of his friends, even if he told them he only wanted to fuck her, Constance, and didn't have any feelings for her at all. According to their theory, when she saw her things were gone, when she realised she'd been really and truly robbed, she burst into tears and couldn't stop crying and she panicked and told him her parents were going to kill her, and so the guy, because he was in love with her, couldn't stand seeing her cry and took her in his arms and threw his buddies under the bus and told her what had actually happened but made her promise she'd never say that he was the one who told *(we never confirmed it, but this does seem the most likely hypothesis).*

'So that same night she went straight to the police and gave their names and the next day they all had to go and apologise. Édouard was beyond scared. I've never seen anyone look so guilty. He went around like a zombie all day thinking he'd be in trouble with the law and then he'd have a criminal record and it would keep him from becoming a teacher, which was his dream.

'But the cops were cool about it, because they knew the boys. They agreed to let it go as long as they returned everything they'd taken. Every last game. It spooked Édouard for good, and when his gang started going out at night with their hammers, he went to meet them less and less because he couldn't get over his fear, even though he tried. It wasn't long before he stopped going out to the toolshed. But so when he saw Reda had taken his things, for him it wasn't such a big deal, I mean it wasn't like he considered stealing awful or weird or unusual, he'd seen other people do it, and not just his gang of freaks, but our big brother, he used to get picked up for shoplifting, so it was nothing new to Édouard. It happened millions of times, and always the same way; the cops came knocking on our door and our mother would open up and as soon as she did, she knew why they were there. They wouldn't know what to do with their hands and they'd look embarrassed when they took off their caps, you could just tell, because they'd known our mother all their lives. They'd grown up in the same village, they saw each other at the café and the news-stand, and they felt bad about having to bring her bad news.'

★

She would know why they were there before they'd said a word. Already she'd be beside herself: 'Don't tell me, what's he done now, oh dear Lord, as if I didn't have enough to worry about, he won't stop till I'm dead from a nervous breakdown, oh God, I've had more than my share,' and then the police would say, as expected, 'It's about your son,' or not 'your son', they'd call him by name because they'd known him since he was a new-born baby, since he'd taken his first steps in the village streets and their children had grown up with him, they'd been schoolmates, first in primary school then in sec-ondary school, until he dropped out, while their children stayed on a little longer because they were the children of police, and often they went on to join the force them-selves; it was as if they'd all been given a single choice, either to steal and be arrested by their schoolmates, or else to become police and do the arresting. 'Your son,' they'd tell her, 'was arrested with a bag full of stolen merchandise, mostly alcohol, at the Carrefour super-market,' and in her devastation my mother would say, 'I know, I know it's not the first time and I'm afraid it won't be the last, I'll be in a wooden box and six feet under and he'll keep at it all the same, oh, what a curse, but listen, he'll pay for this and that's all there is to it, what can I do, I'm so ashamed. I don't know what to do any more, it's such a shame.' And finally, because in the end she couldn't control him, and because she knew she had no power over my brother and knew that he would indeed do it again, and that all the same she would for-give him, treating each new act of delinquency as if it were the last, as if he were on the verge of pulling him-self together, as if he were on the verge of some total and radical rehabilitation, she'd decide she might as well laugh. Before the laughter began, when it was still time to be serious, everyone would tell her she shouldn't stand for it any more, my big brother's behaviour, that she shouldn't put up with his stealing and all the rest of it; they told her not to keep giving him money – the money he demanded, money she didn't have but always found a way to scrape together. 'What do you want,' she'd say, 'he's my kid, I can't let him starve,' even when they warned her that he was spending it on alcohol, that if he had alcohol he'd get drunk and be out of control, and that because he was drunk more or less all the time, he would keep on going into supermarkets and stealing alcohol. And then it would start all over again. But each time she'd say no, this time was the last. She'd say her son had changed, she'd say he wasn't the same man; she'd say, 'He's finished with the booze, that's behind him, he's changed.' He never changed. He'd only start again. And again she'd say, 'That was it, from now on he's done, he swore he was going to quit and this time he means it, I can tell, I know him, he's my son.' And again, he'd start again. I don't know whether she herself believed what she was saying, whether she actually thought that one day he'd quit. In the end she had to laugh, once the anger had passed. 'What's done is done, you might as well laugh, it beats crying,' and so she'd laugh, and she'd mention that he'd been so drunk at the Carrefour he completely ignored the security guards. He took his time, methodically packing the bottles into his knapsack, 'The idiot didn't even take the good stuff, just that rotgut he drinks, you can hardly call it whisky.' She'd make light of it. 'He gave the cameras plenty of time to get it all on film,' and she told us how when he left the Carrefour, where the alarm sensors were out of date and you could just walk out with stolen merchandise, 'he'd stuck so many bottles in his bag, it was like he was bent over backwards, like the hook on a crowbar, like the handle on an umbrella', his bag was that heavy, and she told us it went *clink clink clink* because the bottles kept knocking around inside the bag; every time he tried to shoplift, or almost every time, he was stopped by the guards for some equally cartoonish reason.

'Which is why I think he should have explained all that to Reda, to reassure him. Then Reda would have known how it was and who he was dealing with. Maybe things would have gone another way. He would have seen that Édouard wasn't so different from him, because I'll tell you why he came up to Édouard on the square – well, not the whole reason why, but mainly, it's the way he carries himself, Édouard, I mean, the way he carries himself now but didn't use to. Life is so ironic, when you think about it. It's actually kind of funny.

Édouard goes around in that mask of his, and he plays the part so well that in the end guys like him attack him, they think he's from the other side of the tracks. If he'd told Reda these same stories I'm telling you now, of course it would have reassured him, and things wouldn't have gone the way they did, they didn't need to *(I agree with her. I agree, but doesn't this undermine her theory that the whole thing was planned in advance and immutable — because I know that isn't the case. I have another memory to prove it, namely the look on Reda's face when I took the iPad out of his jacket, the face that replaced his face; I can't remember it in detail, I couldn't draw you a picture, but I do remember the way his face looked, and it was nothing like the determined face he had later on, it was nothing like the face of cold-blooded destruction, because I've seen that face several times in my life, it's a face I know. When I took my iPad away from him, what I saw on his face was surprise, fear, even stupidity — but it was no use explaining this to Clara, a face doesn't prove anything to anyone, not to Clara and not to the police).* But Édouard didn't say anything. All he had to do was explain in simple language, and for fuck's sake it's not exactly hard to understand. If I had been there I would have taken him in my hands. I would have shaken him, I'd have said: Own up, tell him you've stolen things too and it's no big deal, if that's what you really think. If that's what you really think. So what if I don't see it your way, if that's what you really think, then tell him. Tell him about the scrap metal. But the trouble is he'd need to say it right away, and

sometimes Édouard can be so slow. He wasn't exactly con-
ceived in the winner's circle. He doesn't say a thing.

'Instead he takes the iPad out from Reda's jacket. As
if it were nothing. He takes the iPad and puts it on his
desk. He does this not saying a word, mind you. Not a
word. He tells me: In the moment I hoped Reda would
suddenly burst out laughing, that he'd laugh and tell me
it was all a joke and I'd got scared over nothing. I kept
waiting for him to laugh. I was waiting, he tells me, and
all the while thinking, Go on and laugh, Reda, laugh.
What would it hurt you to laugh? But he didn't laugh.

'So what does he do? He asks if Reda had happened
to see his phone. He didn't say: You've taken my phone,
no, the exact words he remembers saying are: You didn't
happen to see my phone, did you? You didn't see me put
it down somewhere, by any chance, it was right there in
my pocket, I saw it there five minutes ago. I was using it
before I got into the shower and now it's not in my
pocket, I'm such an idiot, I know I had it but I can't
think where I put it *(every day I'm less sure about that sentence, maybe I actually did say, Do you have my phone, which
would have meant I was accusing him before I had proof; just
because I'd found the tablet in his jacket, that didn't mean he
had the phone in his pocket. I don't have the courage to tell
Clara this may have been what I said)*. And so the guy gets
mad *(no, he wasn't angry yet, that was exactly the moment
when he hesitated and stuttered, she's forgetting)*, he asks if
Édouard is trying to insult him, if Édouard is calling

him a thief, and Édouard answered: No, but why are you getting so angry? And it's true that getting angry wasn't very bright of him, it wasn't exactly the smartest way to react. It was like an admission of guilt. It wouldn't hurt if it wasn't true. So Édouard said, If you've got it you can give it back and we'll forget it, no big deal, we'll forget it ever happened; he said all he wanted was his phone back. It's just my holiday photos with my two friends Didier and Geoffroy. Because all of a sudden he was fixated on these holiday photos, these souvenirs, the same way he was fixated on getting back home when he ran into Reda on the place de la République.

'So he told himself: I need to get my photos. And at the same time, he was trying as hard as he could to calm the other guy down; he smiled, he made soothing gestures; and now he was starting to actually worry, but still he was nice and polite. It didn't matter. The guy was furious. I mean furious. You couldn't just ask him to tone it down, not like that anyway, he was too far gone. And so what does Édouard do? Does he drop it? Does he give up? Does he let the guy go? Does he open the door so the guy can leave? No, he starts begging *(hearing her say it makes it even more humiliating, how ridiculously I behaved)*, and meanwhile Reda's shouting, he's getting in his face, and Édouard's begging – but he's not begging the guy to go, or even to let him leave, even though it's clear that if they start fighting, the guy's going to kick his arse, Édouard's such a fool, and here he is begging the guy: If you've got my phone, I don't care, I understand – but it's too late for that, it's obviously much too late; Édouard has a quick mind but sometimes he needs everything explained to him, and so what does he do? He talks, and talks, he tells him: So you took the phone, I get it, I would have done the same thing, I totally understand, it was the whatever, the excitement or the adrenaline of stealing, or maybe you need the money, that's completely fine – and he doesn't stop, he doesn't stop, he keeps talking – I just want you to give it back and we'll forget all about it, we'll get together tomorrow the way we said, we'll get something to eat, just the two of us and we won't discuss this and then we'll see each other the next day and we won't discuss it then either, and Édouard tells him: We'll forget all about it, and then we'll forget that we've forgotten – really, that's how he talks, even in front of this guy, he can't help it with the vocabulary, he talks like some kind of politician, it's out of his control, and it must have made the guy even madder, and still he says: If you like, we can pretend it never happened, it's nothing. We'll forget it.'

Reda just stood there while I talked. Not saying a word.

'But it was too late, Reda wasn't listening any more, and he was making a face and yelling, What did you just say to me? What the fuck did you just say to me? And he was so mad he was spitting on Édouard's forehead, and Édouard's face was covered in spit or snot, or maybe both, his face was completely wet with spit, but you get the idea, it was glistening with spit, and the guy's like, What the fuck did you just say to me? He was bellowing, and there was Édouard's face all shiny with his spit. Me, I'd have thrown up. But Édouard, get this, Édouard says it again. He repeats it all over again, as if Reda were asking an actual question: I think you've taken my phone – now he came out and said it – as if "What the fuck did you just say to me?" was a question, I swear to God. He actually answered the question, "What the fuck did you just say to me," for Christ sake, and is it my fault I almost burst out laughing? I feel bad, I know it's serious. But it was all so crazy I thought I was going to laugh and I thought, How on earth could he be so stupid to hear that as some kind of question? I pretended to be chewing on my lip so he couldn't see me smiling, like, "I'm not smiling, I'm just sitting here chewing on my lip," but whatever. The other reason it seems so dumb is because I know what's going to happen. I know what happens next. Hindsight's twenty-twenty, the way they always say; it's easy for me to say I'd have done this and not that. And it's true, here I am acting smart because I know. I'm laughing because I know Reda was a psycho, a psycho on a hair trigger, and if you're dealing with a psycho, there are better ways to act – or you can always try getting the fuck out. But he wasn't actually violent in that moment. All he was doing was yelling.

'But when I say yelling, I mean he was really yelling.

And he said it again, as if it were the only thing he'd ever learned to say, the one and only thing, You're calling me a thief, I'm no thief, you're calling me a thief you insult my mother, you disrespect my mother *(this sort of anxious repetition, which went on much too long, had all the speed, all the marks of improvisation; the same thing happened again at the very end of the night when, after everything, the rape, the strangulation, covered with blood I managed to get him out of the apartment and Reda came back to the door, and pressed his face against the door, I could hear it, I could hear his beard scratching and sliding against my door, and he asked: Are you sure you want me to leave? I feel really bad about this. I'm sorry)*, well, and so Édouard, he told me there was an edge in his voice too, in his own voice, and he couldn't hide it, or what's the word, repress it; so maybe Reda heard that edge in his voice and maybe it made things worse; it's hard to explain, the thing was, he hadn't called Reda a thief, and it bugged him that Reda would keep on saying that; and really, actually, he was hurt. It hurt him that Reda would keep saying, You're calling me a thief. He felt annoyed because that's exactly what he wasn't doing, how many times did he have to say it? Nobody was calling anybody a thief, that's what he was trying to explain, it didn't make him a thief if he'd taken his iPad or whatever else, and he said it in an irritated tone, Now listen – I imagine it was the kind of voice you use with your kid when you're telling him something for the millionth time and he keeps on asking the same question, the way kids do – Now listen, I just got through saying you weren't a thief.

'But by now the other guy can't even hear him. He's just talking on his own: You disrespect my mother, you insult me, you call me – and now he says some words Édouard doesn't understand. The guy is just checked out. And Édouard's saying: It's no big deal, it's no big deal, with Reda saying, "You insult my mother, you insult my family," each one just saying his own thing.

'Then Reda grabbed him. That's what happened, he grabbed Édouard, and what does Édouard do? He stands there like a deer in the headlights. Reda takes the scarf and before Édouard knows what's going on he's wrapped it around his neck. Now Édouard can't move. He's got him broken like a tamed horse, he's got him at his mercy, and the guy winds the scarf around his neck and pulls it tighter, tighter, tighter, until Édouard can't breathe. He cries out, Reda. Édouard had the scarf around his neck – and, and the guy kept pulling it tighter.'

She pauses. Her husband doesn't say anything. I'm tempted to lean in so I can see them through the crack of the open door, but I'm afraid the floor will creak. I stay where I am.

'Excuse me.'

She clears her throat.

'At first he doesn't take it seriously. I mean when Reda puts the scarf around his throat and pulls, the second he does it, he doesn't think he means it. And for that first second, when you can think a million thoughts – at least that's how it seems when you look back, which is what our mother said when I told her – he didn't think he was actually being strangled. He can't believe it. Because until now he never thought of Reda as a thief, much less a killer *(for all I know I didn't think he wasn't a killer, for all I know I didn't think anything at all, for all I know nothing passed before my eyes, no reflection, no memory, maybe my hands gripped the scarf out of a purely reflexive resistance to dying. They say we can never leave language behind; they say language is the essence of being human and that it conditions everything; they say you can't go outside it, for language has no exterior; they say we don't think first and then organise our thoughts into language later on, for language is what allows us to think; they say it is a condition, a necessary condition, of reason and human life – but if language is the essence of being human, then for those fifty seconds when he was killing me I don't know what I was). (And by a strange reversal, today the exact opposite is true, all I have left is language, I've lost the fear, I can say 'I was afraid' but the word can only be a failure, a hopeless attempt to retrieve the feeling, the truth of the fear.)* That first second he told himself this was just a man act- ing a little too rough, but he didn't take it more seriously than that. He grew up rough himself. We all did. He wasn't going to be scared by some scarf around his neck. By some little scrap of cloth. And he must have thought it was a joke – or not a joke, that's not the word, but a warning, I guess, a way for Reda to look tough and impressive, the way men do, because they're idiots. The point being that Édouard would shut up and Reda could walk off with the phone, and go downstairs, and run away knowing Édouard wouldn't call the cops.

'Not that I could ever say any of this in front of Édouard. He can't stand it. However you try to put it, he gets mad and says it isn't true and that you've made it all up. I guess it's too close to the bone.

'So since I know it will only get him worked up, I keep it to myself. But there's no doubt in my mind, if he behaved that way that night, if he was reckless, it's partly because he grew up rough and was taught one too many times not to be afraid. And sometimes that comes out. He can say whatever he likes, it's still there. He's changed less than he pretends. I know I'm right. I've seen how he acts when he comes to visit, the first few days, when he puts his things in his room and acts so prissy. It's like he's trying to prove he's not one of us, he wants us to think he's different – he wants us to think he's new. That he's too good for us. When he gets here, I think he actually lays it on thicker than when he's with those friends of his, Didier and Geoffroy, back in Paris. I'm sure when he's in Paris and he's feeling relaxed he swishes around less than when he gets here and suddenly won't eat meat, because he says meat grosses him out – or then he'll get up and wash his hands every five minutes because he's petted the dog, as if my dog had scabies or fleas when, I beg your pardon, my dog is cleaner than anything they give you in those city restaurants; all that swishing around that city people do, it gets on my nerves, and Édouard does it all. But just you look, two days later and it's a completely different story. He stops queening it up and the act fades away. He calms down, he even starts saying a few words in Picard. He stops saying *Ça va* and starts saying *Cha-vo-ti*, just yesterday after dinner he said *Chétouaite fin bouen*, and maybe he said it for a joke, but still he said it, he stops saying *tomber* and says *tcher*, and he stops being afraid to laugh when some woman, any woman, gets up to go to the toilet and says *Pardon me while I toss my salad*, all the things he used to say before he became a snob, and so he laughs, while in those first days he'll say he doesn't want to hear that kind of talk. He'll say it made him laugh when he was a kid but it's only for kids and now it puts him off his food. He says he's outgrown it. Maybe that's why he always wants to leave so soon. I think he wants to leave because he's afraid of turning back into the kid he used to be. But anyway, as for that night, that's why he acted the way he did. Because he was brought up like we all were, not to take any shit, and if he'd grown up with money you can be sure he'd have got the hell out of there – there's no way of knowing, but I bet.

'The thing is, after four or five seconds with the scarf around his neck, there was no way not to understand. It sank in that this wasn't just somebody acting tough, this wasn't some kind of warning. This wasn't an act, it was murder. The guy was trying to kill him. He realised he was going to die there in his room on Christmas Eve, and Édouard told me how when he thinks back to that moment, to what happened, it feels like he's looking at a photo, he sees Reda standing in front of him and he sees himself sitting on the edge of his bed where Reda made him sit – not by telling him to sit, just by moving towards him so he could strangle him. Reda forced him to sit because he had to take a step back when Reda came at him holding the scarf, and he pulled back and then he was sitting down. Then he finally thought, He's strangling me.'

I did become aware of what was actually going on, and yet the feeling of unreality persisted, and even afterwards, even just three seconds after it ended, the memory was drained of all its reality the way you blow an egg through a hole pierced in the end; in the first second, the memory seemed an hour old, as if it had been, for some reason, transferred, pushed back, projected to an hour before; in the next second, I felt that it had happened several days earlier; by the third and fourth seconds, several years seemed to have risen up between that memory and myself.

'He gave Reda a kick, instinctively. That's when he got those marks, the ones on his neck. The purple marks *(you clumsily tried to camouflage them with an ascot tie that you bought when you first got to Paris, the ascot you stopped wearing years ago when you realised how ridiculous you looked. You had*

*moved to Paris, this was four years ago, and stupidly you wanted
to look like a bourgeois, so as to hide what you saw as your poor
provincial origins — the self you were afraid of, the self your fear
made you see — but your idea of a bourgeois was a hundred years
out of date, precisely because of your distance from that world,
and you'd bought this ascot as well as a three-piece suit that you
wore everywhere, often with a tie, even to go to the supermarket
or to class. Every morning when you put on your out-of-date
clothes, the anxious way you held yourself revealed the past you
were trying so hard to bury; you didn't notice that Parisians and
the children of the bourgeoisie didn't wear that kind of thing; not
ascots, polo shirts and jeans yes, but no ascots; you weren't fooling anyone. One day you finally understood, or rather Didier
pointed it out, and you never wore it again).*

'His temples were throbbing. *Boom boom boom.* The
blood had gone to his brain, it was beating in his head,
and the other guy started in again, Édouard couldn't
stop him: I'm going to take care of your ass, I'm going
to take care of your ass, and *boom boom boom*, You disrespected my mother, I'm going to take care of your ass,
and the blood going *boom boom boom*. And that's what
scared him the most, the shouting *(the noise was the scari-
est part. Ever since that night I can't go looking for a quiet place
without the sense that what I'm doing in fact is trying to escape
the sound of his shouting, as if there were shouting scattered all
around, ready to spring up, as if shouting existed before there
were human beings, and humans were merely tools invented to
give it an outlet).*

'So that's what he needed the most, he needed silence. He needed to make the guy shut up. I asked what he decided to do after he kicked him, and he told me: I dropped my voice. That was his response. I know it's crazy, but there it was: I decided to lower my voice, I needed there to be less noise, so I did the only thing I could do, and what could I do? I could speak softly. So that's what I did. He decided to whisper. He hoped Reda would adjust his own voice, that he'd whisper too – don't ask me where he gets his ideas. While Reda was pacing around the apartment and heading towards the dirty knives in the sink, it seemed to him that if he whispered, Reda would do the same. He could have grabbed a knife, he was shouting, shouting, shouting, it looked like he was about to slice him up. And Édouard responds by lowering his voice.

'What I'll never understand is, it worked. Reda followed his lead. He turned back to Édouard and he did like him. He whispered. I have trouble believing it myself, I'm sorry, it sounds so weird, but that's what he told me, I whispered and I swear he whispered; he came up to me, he walked towards me, and he gently touched my arm and he murmured, under his breath, the way you talk to a kid you're trying to get to sleep; and he could hardly understand what Reda was saying, now that his voice was so soft, now that he was so calm, now that everything about him seemed so calm.'

As Reda walked towards me whispering, I stood up

and in a rush of temerity, I began to speak – not that there was anything especially brave about the way I stood or the words I said, but in that moment I experienced the simple fact of getting up and daring to speak as an immensely difficult and brave act, the only thing I did that entire night that I would call courageous – I told him that this had gone far enough. It was still dark outside. 'It's not too late, you take your things and some money if you want it, leave, and I won't tell anyone, I won't call anyone, I swear, just go home.' That was the kind of thing I said, weak, predictable, cliché, the only things I could think to say; 'You are so young, if you commit a real crime they'll track you down'; and I didn't say the word *police*, just that vague, generalised 'they' in my effort to keep him calm and avoid words that might fuel his anger. I said, 'You'll end up getting caught, everybody does, and you'll ruin your life. They'll put you in jail for life, forever, it's so stupid, do you know what prison is like?' But now he was backing away again: 'You're going to pay, I'm going to kill you, you dirty little faggot, I'm going to take care of your ass, you faggot,' and I thought, *So that's it* – and here's what I thought in the moment, though I'm not so sure today: *He hates himself for wanting men. He wants to redeem himself for what he did with you. He wants to make you pay for his desire. He wants to make himself believe that the two of you did all the things you did, not because of his desire, but as a strategy for what he's doing now, that you didn't make love, but that this has all been part of a theft.*

We adapt quickly to fear. We live with it much more easily than we might suppose. It becomes no more than a disagreeable companion. For a few minutes, maybe less, he alternated between shouts and whispers. More and more, I mastered my fear. He kissed me, he murmured: 'Don't be scared, I'm sensitive, I can't stand it when people get scared or cry.' He stroked my hair. I felt safe, in that moment nothing could harm me, his capacity to reassure me and protect me were proportional to his violence.

There was no escalation of violence. There were these intervals when he grew peaceful, when his attitude changed completely and he was calm and lowered his voice; he murmured, he hesitated, he made promises: 'Everything's going to be okay, there's nothing to worry about.' He kissed my ears, my cheeks, my lips. I spoke to him about his future but that was no good.

Clara described to her husband how desperately I tried to find something else, another vocabulary, another line of argument, since his future meant nothing to him.

'He thought of talking about his family.'

When we first met on the square, he had talked to me about how much family meant to him; I remembered that, and I pretended that my parents' numbers were in my phone – I wanted to get the photos of Didier and Geoffroy, the photos I'd taken with them. I said I didn't know where my parents were living and that I had no other way of getting in touch besides the numbers saved on my phone. Geoffroy told me the next day: 'You should have let him leave with the phone, a phone is nothing.'

Clara remembers this, too:

'His friend Geoffroy told him the next day, You should have let him leave with the phone. A phone is nothing, just a piece of plastic. Meanwhile Édouard doesn't know why, but for some reason he can't let it go about the phone. He starts up all over again asking the guy to give it back. Instead of leaving or changing the subject now that the guy's calmed down, what does he do? He asks for the phone. He won't let it be, but if you ask me it's not really about the phone. That friend of his Geoffroy is way off the mark, but how could he understand? He doesn't know him as well as I do. I'm telling you, it could have been anything, a pencil, a piece of jewellery, or even a person, a hostage, whatever, it would have been the same to Édouard because it wasn't about the phone, it's about these fixations he gets, it's a kind of insanity, no matter what it was, it would have been the same – not for me, mind you, I'd have got the hell out of there a long time ago, but for him *(before the night you met Reda, you would think the way she does, but now you know better; before that night, I had always imagined that if I were facing death, if I were trapped in a burning house or with a murderer, whatever the circumstance might be, I would have done everything I could to extricate myself, that I'd never have given up. I'd thought the imminence of death would have doubled my strength and my courage, would have revealed a power, an ability to shout, to fight, to escape, to run, to defend myself, that even I had never suspected. Of course, in the movies, in newspapers and magazines, I'd seen characters capitulate to their own deaths, and surrender, but I thought I was different, and these images always filled me with a wave of disgust and contempt as I watched them give up the fight so quickly. I thought: I'm much stronger than they are).* It was pure insanity, believe me. He kept on asking and asking for that phone, and I bet he asked for it more than he even let on.'

Maybe I could have made him go away in one of his moments of calm; he would come close to me and – in all my trembling and stammering – I never noticed how many other things he'd slipped into the pockets of his jacket. Over the next month, and even the next day, I found that various things of mine were no longer there, that they'd vanished. I didn't notice that Christmas Eve, in any case they were things that didn't matter, but he really had emptied my apartment, so to speak, and he did it with incredible discretion, since I was sure my eyes had been on him the whole time; I so badly wanted to make the most of his last seconds in my apartment, to admire him while he was in the shower (or rather, I thought my eyes were on him, that's how I remember it even now, though clearly that's not possible or he couldn't have taken all those things). The pockets of his jacket must have been overflowing with my things, a bottle of cologne given to me for Christmas, a watch left behind by a friend, a medallion of the Virgin Mary from when I was baptised, which had just been sitting there in the bathroom ever since I moved in and which of course I never wore but somehow took with me from apartment to apartment, without knowing why I hadn't yet thrown it away.

Then a strange idea occurred to me, the strangest I had that entire night. This is the only scene that I've completely hidden from everyone I've talked to – I hid it from the police, from Didier and Geoffroy, from the nurses, from the doctor at the Hôtel-Dieu, from the strangers I confided in, from that writer, from Clara this week. I've never talked about it, not for reasons having to do with memory or the need to forget certain things, but simply out of shame. I actually remember it much better than the rest of the night; these are the images that remain most vivid and robust, as if what we call shame is no more than memory in its most vibrant and durable form, a superior version of memory, a memory inscribed in the deepest flesh, as if Didier is right and the things we remember most clearly are always those that bring us shame.

There I was in front of Reda. I said to him, 'I tell you what, would you mind helping me look around the apartment for my phone, it seems to have fallen down somewhere. If you don't mind. We could make it a kind of game.' Here is what I suggested: 'Whoever finds the phone, the other one has to give him fifty euros; we'll make it into a contest, just for fun. If you find it, I give you fifty euros. If I find it, you give me fifty euros. Simple.' I swear that's what I said, I can't remember whether I was shaking when I proposed this game, or whether my voice trembled. I was sure the phone was in one of his pockets, I was even more sure that I'd found the iPad in his jacket, and I was certain that he'd pretend to find it if he could have the money. He'd stolen my phone in order to resell it and make a little money; this logic struck me as self-evident, as perfectly simple. The whole time I was thinking about the photos on my phone and how I needed to get them back – or at least, as Clara would have it, I believed that what I wanted was those photos and that phone.

He helped me search. He walked around the apartment, he lifted up the sheets, the blankets. He looked under the bed, under the desk and the chairs, he felt around under the pillows, he stuck his hand inside the pillowcases. He got down on all fours, he put his head down, he looked under the bed.

He wasn't really looking, and you could tell he wasn't looking – that was obvious – but he did the least he could to maintain the illusion that he was going along with our game. He opened the cupboards, he picked up a book, he picked up another book, he took a book off one pile and placed it on another. I did what he did. I mimicked him, I pretended to look, I even inspected the inside of the refrigerator, where sometimes I leave books

or other things by mistake. I pored over the tiny bathroom, and the whole time I kept sneaking looks at Reda.
I could hear the sound of his breathing the entire time.

I never made a run for it. I never went for the door,
even now that calm was re-established. I never tried to
open the door with a quick decisive tug. I never thought,
Get out. I hadn't yet seen the gun in his pocket – so
escape was thinkable, even if it wouldn't have been
exactly easy. What strikes me most of all, now that I try
to remember, is the unreality of the scene, the unreality
of our poses, of our movements. I knew there was nothing to find, and he knew he had the phone, and yet we
searched the apartment from one end to the other; it was
6 or 7 a.m., Christmas Eve was over, and here was
Reda looking through the drawers, and then he'd stop,
he'd think of somewhere he ought to check, or ought to
pretend to check; my face was swelling, it was puffing
up with exhaustion. Now and then, as we combed the
sixteen square metres of the apartment, I would say,
'Any luck?' and he'd say, 'No'; then I would try again:
'Any sign of it?' He answered calmly, the way a person
might answer any normal question. I was barefoot, I was
wearing boxer shorts and a T-shirt. Reda had got dressed
after he took his shower. I didn't dare put on trousers to
cover myself up. I wasn't cold yet. We walked round
and round the studio.

And then he started shouting again.

Interlude

It was in a novel by William Faulkner, *Sanctuary*, that I first found a case like mine, in which a person was unable to flee.

On page 43, Faulkner writes:

Temple backed from the room. In the hall she whirled and ran. She ran right off the porch, into the weeds, and sped on. She ran to the road and down it for fifty yards in the darkness, then without a break she whirled and ran back to the house and sprang onto the porch and crouched against the door just as someone came up the hall.

When I read it, I made this note:

'Today is Tuesday, 11 November 2014. I've just found and read this book by William Faulkner while writing the last pages of *History of Violence*. I'm stunned by my encounter with Temple Drake, by the parallels between us, by thoughts of hers that are exactly identical to my own. Here in the first part of the book, Faulkner is telling the story of a woman, Temple Drake, who after a car accident is taken with her male companion to a ruined house, not far away, inhabited by a small community of men and one woman. One of the men in this community has found her and her companion and has brought them to this frankly troubling house, lost in the woods and underbrush.'

From the beginning, the characters she meets in this house – small-time bootleggers – are presented as violent, unpredictable drunks.

They threaten one another, they fight, they curse, they drink, they threaten Temple, and the possibility of rape – which will take place – hangs over her.

Temple thinks of escaping now and then, although escape will be complicated without a car. She asks the woman who lives in the house to help her. The woman answers that Temple has to get away before it's too late. She insists that Temple go, even though at times she seems to want to keep her there. Several times Temple could do it, she could conceivably get away. Her male companion does manage to leave, in the end, and his example points up the inertia of Temple Drake.

In the scene that I have just transcribed, Temple makes a run for it, and we breathe a sigh of relief, thinking that finally Faulkner will give us the escape scene we've been waiting for, for too long, but no sooner does she escape than she turns round 'without a break', as if in the grip of the situation, as if the first act of violence in this situation was to preclude the idea of an outside, to lock her inside the limits of the situation itself. In chronological terms, the first problem – for her, and for me, too – is not to have been forced into such-and-such behaviour in this interaction, but to have been held *within* the frame of the interaction, within the scene imposed by the situation, that is, in the murky terrain of the bootleggers' house. It is as if the violence of that enclosure, the geographical violence, came first and the other forms of violence merely followed in its wake, as if they were no more than consequences, side effects, as if geography were a history that unfolded without us, outside of us.

And then Faulkner writes:

Temple backed from the room. In the hall she whirled and ran. She ran right off the porch, into the weeds, and sped on. She ran to the road and down it for fifty yards in the darkness, then without a break she whirled and ran back to the house and sprang onto the porch and crouched against the door just as someone came up the hall.

That Christmas Eve, I managed to defend myself from Reda, but only at the last moment, after a long time, and just as it was for Temple, the will to escape, which I ought to have felt the moment Reda lost his temper, was the very last reaction I had.

9

And then all I felt was exhaustion. Clara told her husband that my fear and my pain were suddenly crowded out by the exhaustion that consumed me. Even as I mastered my terror, all I could hear was my exhaustion whispering, *It's time for him to go, it's time for this to end, it doesn't matter how you do it, but it's time for this to end.* I was trying to think.

All of a sudden I was freezing. I'd been so tense this whole time, ever since Reda's transformation, that I hadn't noticed the temperature, but now that I was exhausted I felt how cold it was, my teeth chattered harder and harder, I got goose bumps. My exhaustion was gradually replaced – or rather, reinforced, since the exhaustion remained – by a heightened sensitivity to the atmosphere around me and to my outer body, so that suddenly his scarf was still tightening around my throat, as if it had been around my neck all along, as if he'd never taken it off; it had been ten or fifteen minutes since I'd had anything around my neck, but suddenly I felt the contact of the wool against my throat, coarse and heavy; the sensation, which had gone away, was back. At this point I'd have done anything to make him go away. But now he was the one who didn't want to go. What I remember, too, is that in these moments time doesn't flow the way it normally does. Elements and situations unfolded in a thick fog, as if Reda and I were drunk, as if the world itself were drunk, as if the oxygen and everything in the room were drunk; time flowed differently, more laboriously, more sluggishly, more heavily, the words that came out of our mouths were heavy, tangible, they could have fallen to the floor and shattered into a thousand pieces; our words were distant, as if spoken by other people; our bodies moved in a sort of sticky sludge of inertia, like sand or wool.

While I explained all this to the two police officers, they'd curled up on themselves, backs hunched, hands balled up, they were growing old before my eyes; time once again grew disjointed and each minute took the toll of a normal year.

Reda no longer wanted to leave. And in the midst of his obsessive and unending refrain about his mother, about the family I'd disrespected, he took a revolver from the inside pocket of his jacket. I hadn't seen it before. I don't know whether it was a real gun or a toy, I had no way of knowing, although the male officer came back to this again and again. 'But was it an actual gun? It could have been a toy, you know, that's something we see a lot, a guy uses a fake gun to scare you and push you around, but in this case . . . ,' and I assured him I didn't know; I rebelled against the idea that it was fake, since naturally I saw this as a way of telling me that my fear had been less than legitimate. And the policeman would ask me again: 'But you're sure it was a handgun, you saw it, you remember what colour it was? Can you describe it? It's not so easy to get hold of a gun,' and I thought: *Of course it is. What planet are you living on?* He came back to this with every other question, he asked me so often that in the end I started to wonder, I wasn't sure what I'd actually seen, whether Reda really had had a gun; even though I remembered it, the repetition was eating away at the reality.

The scarf was lying next to the bed. He bent down to pick it up. Without taking his eyes off me. I thought, *He's going to strangle me again.*

He picked up the scarf and he looked at it as if in panic, as if in shock, he looked at the scarf between his fingers as if it might tell him something, as if it might break into speech and whisper what he ought to do. He told me, 'Turn round,' but with so much hesitation I didn't do it, I couldn't take it as an order; I almost thought he hoped I wouldn't obey. But he said it again: 'Turn round,' and I thought, *He wants me to turn my back to him so he can strangle me, he doesn't want to see my face when he kills me.* He said it again: 'Turn round.' I shook my head no, I didn't want to. I stood there and Reda grabbed my right arm. Then he reaches for my left arm, he wants to tie me up with the scarf. I struggle, I won't let him do it, I cry out, but quietly, I was quiet because I didn't want to provoke him, I didn't cry out so much as moan and plead. I resist, he fails to do whatever he's trying to do, he keeps saying over and over, louder and louder, 'I'm going to take care of your ass I'm going to take care of your ass I'm going to take care of your ass.' I was speaking to no one and he was speaking to no one, it seemed as if he'd never get tired but instead would keep on yelling, cursing, meting out and raining down violence for decades, centuries, never letting up; so now I feel all my own energy drain away, with each heartbeat I feel myself losing strength, it's running out, it's leaking from my eyes, my ears, my nose, my mouth; I want to contain it inside me, I can't fight all night, it has to stop; a moment will come when the exhaustion is too much and I'll be paralysed forever. And I thought: *He's not a murderer. You don't just run into murderers on the street. Murderers aren't skinny Kabyles. They're menacing and you don't just happen to meet them by chance. He's not built like a murderer . . . What about him could mark him as a murderer? A hand, a foot, an arm, a face?*

I hoped someone, a neighbour, would hear us and intervene. But nobody came. He was still trying to tie my arms, he still had the scarf in his hands. Since this wasn't working, he grabbed the gun, which he'd slipped back into the inside pocket of his fake leather jacket; he drops the scarf on the floor or else he wraps it around his own neck, I don't remember, and he pushes me down on the bed, crushing my face against the beige fabric of my sheets; I can smell the more or less realistic peach scent of the detergent. When he was raping me, I didn't cry out because I was afraid that he would shoot me. I held still. I breathed through the mattress; the oxygen tasted of peach. His pelvis pounded against me with a dull, dry sound. I focused on the taste of peach. I told myself a real peach wouldn't taste like that, wouldn't taste the way that smelled. All around us was silence, always the same silence. I had to struggle somewhat. I needed to handle him carefully if I wanted to avoid what seemed to me the worst. What he really wanted was my non-consent. He was on top of me, but he materialised in everything around me; I gather this is a recurring motif in accounts of rape: everything became an extension of Reda, my pillow was Reda, the pitch darkness was Reda, the sheets were Reda.

I struggled in order to reassure him, my cries were swallowed up by the thickness of the mattress. I needed to maintain a delicate balance, to struggle without struggling too hard, to get rid of him without doing it too quickly. My cries were partly from pain, but if I'd actually put up a fight it would have provoked him more, and so I planned out every flinch, every groan; I did what I could to muffle any groans of actual pain, letting him hear only the groans I faked, I used the internalised force of the actual groans to produce the fake ones, and I focused on my train of thought: *No one has ever seen a peach that smelled like that, this is not the scent of a peach but the idea of the scent of a peach.* I struggled harder to give him pleasure, more pleasure, and so to end it sooner. I controlled everything, I measured everything – at least that's what I wanted, and what I told myself to do.

The policewoman said if it had been her she'd have shouted as loud as she could.

Just then, his body trembled and convulsed, his cock contracted, I felt it stiffen and grow, it hurt me more; during his orgasm he would be weak, less vigilant, I could get away. And at that moment, the exact moment of his orgasm, I elbowed him in the side. This wasn't bravery on my part, it was just a gamble.

He didn't see it coming. He was surprised, disconcerted, and he tumbled sideways off the bed, like an insect flipped over on its back, helplessly waving its tiny legs; now suddenly off balance, with his trousers around his knees, he looked like a lost and hunted beast, with his cock still stiff as a rod, covered in blood, erect and suddenly ridiculous, just a pinkish bit of flesh clumsily attached to the middle of his body.

I ran to the door. From my bed to the door is less than two metres. I was on the landing, almost naked, blood running down my thighs in long sinuous red lines, when he caught up to me; he'd pulled up his trousers but the buttons of his fly were hanging open. He didn't take me back inside. He could have, easily enough, he only needed to threaten me with the gun. He stood facing me, paralysed. Again I saw the fear in his eyes, but bigger now, bigger than ever, as if it were a ghost that passed between us, between my eyes and his. He stood facing me on the landing, baffled, as if blinded by his own ineptitude. Maybe he felt regret. He had no idea what he should do, or could do, he looked stunned by his fall and by this brutal turn of events. He was a pathetic creature, feverish and dazed. Not that I felt any pity towards him. It's not as if I was touched by this sudden weakness of his; it didn't make me feel sad, but it didn't make me feel glad or triumphant either. The only question, I told the police when the interview ended, the only question in my mind was: How to do it? And I told Reda: 'Get out or I'll scream.' When I came to this part of the story with the police officers, they didn't believe me. 'That's it? That's all it took?' And I said, 'Yes, that one little sentence panicked him.' Reda froze. His face went rigid, he said, 'Please don't.' My apartment door was open, he took a few steps towards the doorway, he leaned over, he reached down to pick up his jacket, which was near the landing, and I watched him leave, backing his way around me, as if he were nervous and even afraid. I knew he wouldn't try anything else. It was over.

I went back inside, I closed the door. Then Reda came back. He pressed his face against the door, I could hear him, and he said, 'You're sure you want me to leave? I feel bad about this. I'm sorry.' I answered: 'Go.' It was over.

The policeman could hardly believe it, I told Clara that the next day the policeman could hardly write down what he'd just heard, he couldn't believe that was the end of the story; the end couldn't be so flat, so anti-climactic and disappointing, and he asked me, 'What happened then?' as if there had to be something more. 'I stayed in my apartment. Looking back, I say I knew it was over, but the truth is I thought he might come back. I locked myself in my studio and I waited. I sat on the bed, there was blood all over the sheets and on the floor.' I thought of AIDS. I had to go and get emergency treatment. But what if Reda was in the stairwell. What if he was hiding and waiting for me to come out. I sat there, doing nothing, just hating him; I sat and hated him for a while, then I decided to go. I took a shower – or no, that was later, when I got back from the hospital. I put on some clothes and I walked to the hospital; I think I took an umbrella but didn't use it. In my pocket I had a utility knife for protection, in case Reda was hiding and waiting. It was raining outside, the clouds were like chunks of cement, and it was that sort of very fine drizzle, microscopic and clammy, that covers your face and soaks through your clothes. I walked to the hospital in the rain. It took me a while to find the emergency room. That peach scent, I told myself, was absurd. At the hospital in the waiting room I saw a homeless man, he was pacing back and forth.

10

She had to stop working when they had their first kid. She said: 'With the work they had me doing I'd just as soon stay home.'

Her husband remains silent, mysteriously silent, and I ask myself why he hasn't said a word since he came home. At first when she started talking I assumed it was fatigue, since he'd been working all week, or maybe it was just his usual shyness and silence – unless that shyness and silence were just the sharp edge of his role as a man in the village (manhood being associated with taciturnity, at least in the presence of a woman or child), and then there was his job, driving a tractor-trailer for a big corporation, which is to say, a job that's had him on the road for the last ten years, by himself, with no one to speak to for five or six days at a time.

He's spent more than ten years on the road all over Europe and into Asia, with no company except the TV built into the cab of his truck, and he's covered a lot of highway; he travels thousands of kilometres per week, with nothing before him but the same strips of concrete and the same road signs, all exactly alike except for the names of the cities, which in any case he never visits – when and how would he have the time? – and which for him are only strings of letters and names of warehouses, or at the most they signify different figures, since his salary depends on the distance between each city and France – Berlin meaning an extra hundred euros on the cheque he gets each month, Kracow meaning two-fifty, Riga four hundred, and so on, and just like today he never speaks a word; he has neither the chance nor the urge to speak, without the chance he never gets the urge unless it's to order a cup of coffee in the middle of the night or acrid wine in a cardboard box from a sleep-deprived vendor at a service area on the highway, all alone with the smell of his own body filling the truck, a strong scent, sweated out over nights of sleep and meals in the confined space of the cab.

One time I went with him to London. I was twelve, and he invited me along. He'd be gone two days and one night. I said yes, thinking that I would discover a country that wasn't France and that I'd finally get to practise the few words of English I'd learned at school. I went with him, but the deeper we drove into England the clearer it became that we weren't going to hear a word of English, that we wouldn't see a single street or town; we would only follow our route through a series of nameless suburbs until we reached a big warehouse where my sister's husband unloaded his freight, emptying his truck without speaking to the English workers, whom he'd call *les Rosbifs*, he didn't even bother to say hello, only *bonjour*, and turning aside to me he said, 'I'm French and I speak French.' The only thing I've retained from that trip we took was the fact of his solitude and his sadness, and the vision of his body as he lay beside me in the cab.

She goes on with the story; he doesn't speak. She says it was just after seven when I walked through the automatic doors of the Hôpital Saint-Louis. It was deserted. It had been less than an hour since Reda disappeared.

I'd told her about the hospital that morning of 25 December, how muffled and calm it was, and Clara explains that a nurse appeared after twenty minutes. She walked over to me, she was tall and elegant, and she handed me water in a little white translucent plastic cup. I started to cry. I told her my story several times, and I cried. She showed no sign of impatience or annoyance; she remained serene, professional, imperturbable. 'You were very brave. And what you went through is like facing death.' She asked whether I had any family I wanted to call; I told her no. When she stepped out of the examination room, I don't remember why, but I rubbed my fingernails against the raised circles on the plastic cup; I had an urge to scream, and although I did all I could to master it, I had an impulse to overturn every piece of furniture in the room, a violent impulse to write on the walls, to tear the sheets, to run wild and sink my teeth in the pillows and shake my head from side to side until they tore open and the feathers came out and drifted across the room, I wanted to see them falling gently over my head and shoulders – and then to see the terrorised face of the nurse when she walked back in.

The nurse told me that a doctor would be with me momentarily, in just a few minutes, slightly longer than the usual waiting time; 'Obviously,' she said, because it was Christmas morning and they were short-staffed, 'doctors have a right to their holidays, too,' and I acknowledged what she said, I would wait. 'Can I bring you anything else?' I didn't need anything. I thanked her profusely, I went on and on. I thanked her for letting me live. There was nothing I could do now but wait; I went so far as to say: 'I'm so lucky to have walked in and found someone like you.'

There was graffiti on the walls of the examination room, drawings, a sentence here and there, and as I lay there on the dusty bed, which creaked whenever I made the slightest movement, I wondered who exactly had the time to do that, who overcame the fear of getting caught, who had overcome the fear that the doctor might come in and catch them in the act. I'd never have been so bold. But no one came, the doctor never appeared despite what the nurse had promised. I complained in a tone that was soft and smiling and was meant to sound threatening; I crossed the corridor and told them, 'I'm afraid I can't wait much longer.' Then I went back and waited. I got up and walked around in circles, round and round and round – then I had to go and throw up. I told the nurse in the office across the hall, where I had now been several times, that I was sick to my stomach, I said, 'If the doctor comes I'm in the men's room,' but what I thought was: *Because of you. I have to go and throw up because of you. I'm sick because of you, because you're leaving me to die.*

In the men's room, standing across from the sink with his greasy hair plastered down over his forehead and across his face, there was the homeless man. He was leaning down and had his head underneath the automatic hand dryer, which was blasting hot air. Clara describes him: bent over, head under the machine. He opened his mouth and let the air in so it puffed out his cheeks, deforming them, the way a kid will stick his head out of the window of a speeding car, the way I liked to do until I was twelve or thirteen when I went for a ride with my father; the homeless man opened his mouth, revealing a chaos of black and yellow teeth, though really it was more like a series of little brown rocks, like a chain of tiny mountains, their jagged slopes separated by great empty arid spaces where once upon a time there must have been other teeth. He let out a few small groans of pleasure, he sighed. He didn't notice me standing there. I rinsed out my mouth, still coated with vomit, in one of the sinks. I lifted my head. I saw myself in the mirror, my eyes were a brighter blue than usual, 'I found them beautiful,' I told Didier and Geoffroy that same night; I spat a few bits of yellowish slime into the drain while he, in a world of his own, went on with his long lament, drunk on the warm air in his mouth. On his way out he smiled at me. I saw his teeth again, I imagined him biting into a piece of raw meat, the blood on his chin and lips. Ten minutes later I was back in the examination room. Still no doctor. In my impatience, I tightened my jaw and my fists, I thought: *Now it's too late, you're sick, you're sick because of them*, I got up and started walking around the room in circles again. *Now it's too late.*

Clara says:

'He went across the corridor. He wasn't going to tell them again.'

She says I went back to the room across the hall, I didn't realise the doctor was sitting right there. Once more I asked when the doctor was going to arrive, and the other nurse at the back of the office – whom I'd never spoken to but who had been there the whole time, at least I thought she was the other nurse, the one who hadn't introduced herself and whom I automatically thought of as the other nurse, whom I had baptised 'the other nurse' in my conversation with myself – now spoke to me, explaining that she was the doctor: 'I'll be right with you.' She had been there all along; they'd asked me to be patient, they had told me the doctor was on the way and that it was taking longer than usual because it was Christmas, and now I realised that the doctor had been there from the very beginning; since the moment I stepped into that phantom hospital she'd been sitting here in this office, across the hallway from the room with the graffiti, just a few metres away; she was playing solitaire on her computer while, inside my body, with every passing second, the AIDS was probably germinating and had begun to wreak its pitiless destruction on my immune cells.

She saw me after I'd been waiting in anguish for more than an hour; she didn't apologise, she didn't say she was sorry, she didn't seem embarrassed that her colleague had lied. 'You are Monsieur Bellegueule, yes?' She told me I had a funny name, and once she'd made this tasteless remark, I replied coldly that it was no longer my name. I wanted to be done with her as quickly as possible. I counted: *Count to five hundred and you'll be done with her.* She sat facing the computer, a few steps from the bed, and before she could even ask the first question, I interrupted. I had to tell her the thing I'd been afraid of all morning – that if I died they would inform only my family in the most restricted sense, my biological family, the ones on my birth certificate, I was terrified that no one would tell Didier or Geoffroy or any of the other friends I live with here in Paris, having left that other family far behind.

11 (details of a nightmare)

Clara didn't know about this either: the horrid vision I had of my own funeral, probably inspired by another Christmas present from Didier, Claude Simon's novel *The Acacia*, though in any case I guess it's natural to imagine one's own funeral; Geoffroy says everybody does, at least once, and I don't know whether to feel ashamed that I'm so ordinary or relieved that I'm not abnormal. In any case, I told her – I told the nurse – about this nightmare of mine, where everyone who mattered to me would be absent, while the actual audience would have been absent from my life – various cousins who wouldn't be able to understand the circumstances of my death, who would ask the same questions as the policeman: 'But why would he take a stranger up to his apartment in the middle of the night, what was he thinking, the person must have forced his way in, he had to have forced his way in or something happened that we don't know about, nobody takes a stranger up to his apartment in the middle of the night, it doesn't hang together, I'm telling you it doesn't hang together,' or worse, in the same vision, some of the men would say, 'I'm going to kill that dirty Arab who killed him, I'm going to skin him alive, I'm going to tear his balls off,' and other men would say, 'I always told him, Be careful, but what's the point, he never listened, he was such a little know-it-all,' and the men who knew, or at least who knew a little more than the others, would take the shameful secret to their graves, because the truth about how I died wasn't something they could talk about at work or in the village; instead they'd say, 'He was killed, he was attacked, it was an Arab, he was strangled by that filthy son-of-a-bitch Arab' (since anyone from beyond Spain is an 'Arab' – the Portuguese, Greeks, even the Spanish themselves), 'but you couldn't tell him anything'; they'd never say 'He took a guy home with him' or 'He met another guy like him on the street' for fear of betraying themselves.

And the village women, in the little village square, in the square surrounded – surrounded and defined – by the church, the town hall and the school, in the square where the women went to gossip, they wouldn't be fooled. 'Le sienne Bellegueule (*le sienne* meant the son or the daughter of. I was often called *le sienne Bellegueule*, that is, the son of Bellegueule – my father – just as my brothers were sometimes called *le sienne Bellegueule* and my sisters were called *le sienne Bellegueule* and even my father, in the presence of older people from the village who'd known him

143

since he was a boy, was called *le sienne Bellegueule*), le sienne Bellegueule, don't you know, he was killed by an Arab he brought home so they could mess around, I always said he was that way, and then to take home an Arab . . . What did he think was going to happen! May he rest in peace! Poor boy, he didn't deserve a thing like that, he always did so well at school and was so polite, he always said hello, always, when you saw him at the bakery, he was never rude, he always made a point of saying hello. Even if he was on the other side of the street, he'd always wave, sometimes he'd even cross just to say hello,' and meanwhile in Paris, Didier and Geoffroy would have no idea where I was. I told the nurse: they'd have no way of knowing I was dead, they'd wonder why they hadn't heard from me in three days, when usually we exchanged a few dozen or even a hundred texts and emails every day; they'd come and knock on my door, they'd enquire with the caretaker, but they wouldn't get any answers. They'd find out what had happened only after the funeral, and then it would be too late. And in my nightmare – I could just see it – they'd have to take a taxi from the Abbeville station, once they'd got off the train from Paris, because it's another seventeen kilometres by car across fields of rapeseed, sugar beet and potatoes, and there they'd be at this unfamiliar station, in this unfamiliar country. Geoffroy would be clutching an impressive bunch of flowers, which he'd have just bought from the florist opposite the station (no matter if Didier said,

'Why buy flowers when he's dead, flowers he'll never see'), flowers he'd have bought from a helpful, smiling, raw-handed little woman, with whom they'd have exchanged a few words, and inevitably, in the little station, where he and Didier would be waiting for the taxi, everyone would stare at Geoffroy because of the great big showy bouquet, not to mention the loud crinkling of the cellophane it had come wrapped in, and inevitably he would start to feel like a fool. He would have bought a towering, an absurdly big bouquet, 'he always loved that sort of thing' (it all sounds so ridiculous out of context, without the emotional charge that gives it life – but it's only funny from a distance). The two of them would engulf themselves in a taxi, if only to get away from the onlookers, who would wonder what that odd pair of men were doing there, looking so out of place; in a little working-class village like that one sees so few Parisians, they look like clowns in their overcoats, with their little round glasses, waiting for a taxi, because nobody ever takes a taxi, it's too expensive – unless it's for medical reasons in which case the government will reimburse you – and they wonder: 'What on earth are those two freaks doing here?' and some, one imagines, might observe them with compassion; compassion is not at all out of the question, especially when it comes to the women, who were brought up to be more compassionate, and have learned to empathise more easily, and are more intelligent – they may be touched, guessing that these must be flowers for a funeral, that these are friends who have come all the way from the city for a funeral. The two men would finally install themselves in the taxi, which would take them to the village cemetery, but in the taxi they'd be cramped by the immense, the unaccommodating bouquet, and exasperated by the driver, who would be smoking – because here, so far from the centres of things, so far from any big city, so far from political life, one is also far from any health codes – so there they'd be, crammed inside a taxi with a chain-smoking driver and Didier gasping for breath, since he can't stand cigarettes and never could, but not saying anything because he doesn't dare. Maybe they weep, or maybe their throats are too tight, too pinched and dry, for them to share anything beyond the scraps of their quiet grief, and each time one says the same few words, the other nods almost invisibly and offers a gentle mm-hmm.

Then they arrive. After forty-five minutes in the taxi they pull up outside the cemetery, and the driver – who has thought of nothing else this entire time, who has been staring at these two in his rear-view mirror, and screwing up his nerve, and persuading himself that these two Parisians won't give him any trouble – the driver demands an outrageous, a truly indecent fare considering the distance they've travelled, seventeen kilometres. He gets so few fares he has to work a second job on the side; driving doesn't pay the bills; so why, he asks himself, should he hesitate to overcharge a couple of Parisians, why should he go without; it's normal, it's a kind of wealth redistribution; and besides, he hates these *Parigots*, you don't know whether to laugh or look away (he remembers the playground taunt *Parigots têtes de veaux, Parisiens têtes de chiens*). Didier pays without a word. He knows the driver is cheating him, but he can't be bothered to argue. They get out of the cab and walk through the mud, with each step in the puddle-soaked earth their shoes release brown flights of bubbles. It's raining, obviously – it's the North – and the unending rain beats down on their faces and lends the scene an even more pathetic air; they open a little rusted steel gate, which you can tell used to be deep green before the paint flaked off (the rain, always the rain). When they close it behind them it gives a sharp squeak, a rusty sound, and they walk on side by side without exchanging a glance or a word, heads lowered in search of a name hidden among the concrete markers, most of them neglected and covered with ivy and moss. The grave is there, invisible under the flowers left by the village women ('Poor boy, and so young too'), so they can't find any place to put their bouquet and they leave it on a neighbouring grave, what can you do. 'To think we weren't there,' they keep saying, 'to think we missed the funeral.'

12

She had changed. The moment she realised why I was there, her voice had changed. Every time she addressed me, she looked away – she turned towards the computer screen, which cast a purple glow over her cheeks.

'What I told Édouard is maybe she kept you waiting because she thought how serious could it be if every two minutes you kept walking back into her office. Opening the door and closing the door, opening, closing, getting up, lying back down. She must have thought you were possessed – or had ants in your pants at any rate. Or maybe the intake guy never told anyone you were there. You should never be rude to the intake people, they're the worst. Maybe the nurse didn't say anything either.

'So he tells her the whole entire story. But he says he isn't going to file a police report – but why did he go into all that then, why all the detail? What's the point? Anyhow, she tried to change his mind.'

But I refused. At first she pushed back: she told me that

the legal procedures were there to help me, that they existed for my benefit, and I thought, *How can anyone actually believe these procedures do anyone any good?* What I thought was, *I'm afraid*, but what I said was, 'I'm not interested.' What I thought was, *I'm afraid he'll come back and take revenge*, but what I said was, 'I don't want to,' and I added that I had political reasons for not wanting to file a report – which happened to be true, even if those weren't the main reasons – that it was because I hated repression, the very idea of repression, because I thought Reda didn't deserve to go to prison. But most of all what I thought was, *I'm afraid*. She acted as if she hadn't heard me, she kept looking at the screen with her purple-and-fuchsia face; she must have learned long ago, over years of experience, that her real job was to manage these moments of silence and wield them against the insanity of her patients. She handed me the prescription and reminded me that I could still change my mind the next day. When she first turned on her computer she had told me, 'I see you've come for this medication once before.' It was true; I had taken a preventive medication for AIDS two years before. The moment after she said it, she winced: 'There's nothing wrong with that, of course' – and her *nothing wrong with that* meant that something was indeed wrong, that something was wrong with me; she'd said it a little too fast and a little too loud, as if someone had just said the opposite, or as if she'd had to chastise an orderly who'd called out, who had shouted, 'There's something wrong with this guy over here,' as if an orderly had got up on a desk or a hospital bed, made a trumpet with his hands, and started shouting for everyone to hear, that there was something wrong with me; she'd said, 'There's nothing wrong with that,' I told Clara, defensively, to overcome her first thought, her first reaction, the first thing that came to her mind, and she was struggling inwardly to think something else, or to forgive herself for what she hadn't said but had thought: she said what she said precisely because she'd thought the opposite and wanted to redeem herself through speech.

Clara says the doctor and I rose to our feet, she opened the door for me and we walked down the corridor past the perfectly matched hospital doors, nearly all of which were shut.

The lights in the hospital were low, Clara says. The doctor's heels clicked against the laminated floor. The sound suited the twilight of the corridors, as if the sound emanated from the gloom; she led me to the elevator, and she said, 'Go down to the basement and take the second corridor to your left. Basement, second corridor to the left. There you'll find the hospital pharmacy, and they'll give you the medication.' And then: 'You still have plenty of time to file a report.'

Clara:

'She was right, you had to do it.'

We said goodbye, I pressed the down button for the elevator, I thanked her and turned away.

I stepped out of the elevator. There in the basement the silence was even more striking than it had been upstairs. For a second, maybe more, it seemed to me that I was all alone in the hospital and that even the doctor had slipped away once I turned my back, that everyone had hurried off, but in a silent kind of hurry, without telling me, that I had been left behind and would spend the rest of my life wandering this maze of corridors. I looked for the pharmacy. I could hear noises but they all seemed to be so far away that I might have spent hours trying to find them, running this way and that, and still never reached them, never come near them, never grasped them or touched them. All the corridors looked alike. I found the pharmacy, they gave me some capsules that I put in my pocket, and I left.

I got home and sat down on the bed. I kept telling myself, *Now there's nothing left to do.* I was numb with time. *Now you don't even know what to do with yourself.* I checked the time on my iPad and waited. Geoffroy told me that's a normal reaction, that after everything's revved up, it takes a while to come back down; once again, it felt as if my body was a step behind reality, which had already started to change. That's when I cleaned my apartment and went to do the laundry.

'After he did the laundry he came home and opened the window. He thought it would help purify the place, to air it out – whatever, he wasn't in his right mind, he thought he needed to let in new air that Reda hadn't breathed. So he stands at the open window, he holds on to the curtains, and he blows out as hard as he can. He breathes. He made himself cough just to get rid of the air that was moving around inside him. He was worried about where the oxygen came from, if you see what I mean. I made myself cough, he told me, because I was convinced the air in my lungs was the same air Reda had inhaled and exhaled and now I had inhaled it and so on, and now it was all just sitting there in my lungs. Naturally he couldn't have that, Reda's air in his lungs. So there he stood at the window getting rid of the air, breathing, spitting, and coughing.'

Henri was already up. When I turned on my iPad I'd seen a little green dot next to his name on Facebook; I'd sent him a message. He invited me over, and after my second message, saying I didn't want to intrude – which obviously he didn't believe – I walked to the closest bike station, got on a bike and went to his apartment. I pedalled in the cold, eyes tearing, knuckles red on the handlebars. Didier and Geoffroy were still asleep.

I got to Henri's place and we lay down on the bed; I told myself I should make love to him, I was about to beg him to make love to me, as one more way to rub out the trace of Reda, so that Reda wouldn't be the last person this had happened with. I thought it would be another step towards his liquidation; I didn't want 'Reda was the last person I slept with' to be a possible sentence, and I wanted to make it impossible right away.

Geoffroy wrote to me a few hours later. I was lying there beside Henri with my eyes closed. It was around noon.

'Naturally they couldn't meet up at the place de la République,' Clara says. I left Henri's apartment, I thanked him. He said, 'I'm here for you any time, day or night.' I waited for Geoffroy alone at a bus stop near the Gare de l'Est. Each time I saw a face come out of the metro, or a cab, or through the doors of the station behind me, I thought: *He's found me.* I had to stare at the face for a long time before I could be sure it wasn't Reda: I saw him everywhere, that morning every face was his, and even if the person rising up from the metro looked nothing like him, even if it was a woman or a much taller man – Reda wasn't tall – it took a long time for my heart to stop racing and for Reda's face, which I plastered on every face I saw, to disappear, to fade, to dissipate, to evaporate, and for me to see the real face of the person walking towards me.

Clara goes on, she says I looked at the clock above the bus stop – and I thought: *Hurry, Geoffroy, hurry, I'm counting to one hundred and twenty-five and if you're not here by the time I get to one hundred and twenty-five it means Reda's going to find me.* He didn't come. *Now I'm counting to ninety-two and this time if you don't show up, then it's definite, this time it's for sure, Reda's going to find me.* And then he did come. We took a taxi to go meet Didier; Geoffroy said he'd pay for a taxi because it was faster and he'd guessed I'd be afraid of running into Reda in the metro. In the taxi we tried to talk about other things, but words kept changing their meaning; a kind of coded language did the talking for us; he asked what I'd like to have for lunch and suddenly *lunch* meant 'scarf', he asked the driver to turn up the radio and suddenly *music* meant 'gun', *Didier* meant 'Reda'.

13

Didier was waiting at Le Select. He was wearing the sweater I'd given him the night before, I could see it from far away; he was sunk in the banquette at the back, behind the coat racks, with a cup on the table before him. He looked distressed – this distress, which was once a solace, has since become unbearable. Towards the end of a documentary Clara and I watched yesterday on Channel Five, a voice-over mentioned the rapes committed against black women during the days of slavery; when the voice-over said the word *rape* I could feel Clara's embarrassment, I saw her mouth tighten, her eyes narrow, and I hated it, I hated her distress, the way it forced me back into the past, I thought: *She will never understand that, as much as I cling to my story, it is also the thing that seems furthest from me and the most foreign to what I am; she can't understand that I clutch it to me for fear it will be taken away, but that all I feel is disgust, the deepest disgust, if someone comes to me and whispers that it's mine; the moment they remind me, I want to cast it into the dust and leave it behind.*

Didier urged me to talk. He told me to talk as much as I needed to, but to move on as quickly as I could to another topic – not to forget, no, for forgetting wasn't possible, and even if it were, that might not be something to wish for, but in any case it wasn't; and he was right, I know from experience that the isolation of those who try to forget the past is as terrible as the isolation of those for whom the past is an obsession; I've learned that the question is never whether or not to forget, that this is a false dichotomy; the only question, as I told Clara later – this week actually, almost a year later – the only question is how to remember the past without repeating it, and since that night of the twenty-fourth, or rather the next day, that's what I've tried to do, just as I promised Didier: I've been trying to construct a memory that would let me undo the past, that would amplify it and destroy it, so that the more I remember and the more I lose myself in the images that remain, the less they have to do with me.

But the next thing Didier said was: 'You have to file a report with the police.' I didn't want to. I focused on the details of the sweater he was wearing; he was already wearing it, out of kindness I knew, for my sake, to show me how much he valued my gift. I told myself it looked good on him. I wanted to tell him I thought that colour suited him, he ought to wear it more often. He said

again: 'You have to file a report.' And I didn't understand. After what he'd just said, he was contradicting
himself, and it made me very angry, I hated him. This
had never happened before. Geoffroy was more reserved,
more hesitant; for several months he'd been writing a
book on the justice system, *a critique of judgment*, which
would be called *Judge and Punish*, we discussed his book
practically every day, I knew more or less what was in it,
and for that reason I assumed he would defend me. I
expected him to be on my side, but in the end he said it
was important, important that I go and file a report, despite all his reservations, and I thought, *Important for
whom?* I thought: *In any case, you can't send someone to
prison, you can't do that, you're not capable of that* – I had no
ally, no support, but my own arrogance, I looked around
me and that was all I had, I seized it, I clung to it, and I
thought: *They don't know what prison is actually like, but I
do, I've seen a prison, they never have, they don't know, you
went to visit your cousin Sylvain in prison and you remember,
you remember everything, he told you how they lived; and he's
not the only one. He's not the only one. You've seen the worn,
ravaged, lacerated faces of the other prisoners, the devastated,
ravaged faces of the families leaving the jail, ravaged as if they
were trying to share the burden, but these two don't know, they
can't know, they haven't seen* – arrogance, come to my rescue –
*they haven't seen, but I remember clearly, they've never seen the
prison gate, they don't know what they're talking about, they
haven't seen the brick wall, they haven't seen the shadow of the*

wall, they haven't seen the families lined up before the wall, begging and grovelling, waiting for the guard to call their name, waiting to file inside. But I restrained myself and kept from speaking. I said Reda would find me after he got out of prison, if they arrested him, he would hunt me down and take revenge, and Didier answered, 'But that never happens.' He said Emmanuel had once explained to him that this never actually happened, and Emmanuel knew because he was a lawyer, 'he knows more about it than you do', he was an expert and he said this sort of revenge didn't exist. I looked down at Didier's cup, where it was sitting in front of me, and I thought: *But that doesn't make my fear any less real, that doesn't make me feel less overwhelmed, and they should be worrying more about your fear and less about probabilities, and they should be thinking of your fear above all else, but they're not, they're not, they're not thinking of you or your fear,* and I said none of this out loud, obviously I said nothing, all I said was that I didn't want this business to stretch out for months and months. I explained that if there were a trial I'd have to go over it again and again, that what had happened would become that much more real, that what had happened would inscribe itself that much more deeply in me, in my body, in my memory; I had no idea how badly I'd want to talk about it later on, I couldn't have guessed that the way I'd spoken to the nurse that morning prefigured the person I'd become over the next few weeks – not that this had any bearing, since being allowed to speak of a thing and being obliged or summoned to speak are utterly separate things, are as different as they can be. I now know that these two things we call 'speaking' have nothing in common, that sometimes what we call speaking is more like suffering, or being silenced, or throwing up; I know today that language lies; and Didier replied that I would forget much more easily if I filed a report; I thought: *That's not true and he knows it, they want to lock you up inside a story that's not your own, they want you to carry around a story you never asked to have, it's not your story, and that's what they've been telling you since you sat down, that's what they keep saying: file a report, because that's what they want, they want you to bear witness, they want you to bear it on your back and if you spend a few months bent double under its weight, tough luck for you, tough luck if it breaks your bones, tough luck if this story is too much to bear, tough luck if it cracks my ribs, splits my skin, tears my joints, and crushes the organs inside me*, and Didier and Geoffroy kept talking, only now I couldn't understand what they were saying, I was so furious I couldn't even see them, I only felt them as admonitory shadows beside me; they were no longer Didier and Geoffroy, they were no longer the two people who had saved my life so many times; those two had ceased to exist, and I thought: *They're just like Reda. They are Reda. If Reda is a name for the moment when you had to endure what you never wanted to endure, if Reda is a name for deprivation, for silence, for your disappearance, if Reda is a name for the time when you had to do what you never wanted to do, to cross a line you never wanted to cross, to be what you never wanted to be, then you don't see the difference, try as you might, I thought, I don't see the difference, try as I might, they are only extensions of Reda, they are Reda, I had stopped looking at them or trying to make out their faces and I thought: They are Reda, they are Reda, if that night Reda took away your movement, if what Reda took away was your freedom, your freedom of movement, the freedom of your body, they are doing exactly the same thing, and you're begging them for mercy the same way you begged him for mercy. You're begging them to stop but they won't, they're strangling you, they're suffocating you and no matter how you beg them to stop, they won't.* And Didier said: 'If you don't file a report, he'll do it to someone else, he'll do the same thing to someone else, and you have a fundamental duty of solidarity to protect every—' *But why should I have to pay? Haven't I been through enough?* and I kept quiet, *He has his own interests at heart, not yours,* and then I thought, *No, not even, he has nothing to gain if you file a report, what's he got to gain? Nothing. He's repeating what he's been taught but he hasn't even got anything to gain* – and Geoffroy went after me, he assailed me, he drowned me under the weight of the story I wanted nothing to do with, he plunged my face in the mud I'd been trying so hard to escape, he insisted: 'You got lucky, but the next one will get killed—' *But you're not the one who'll have to pay, you don't have to pay all over again, you don't have to sacrifice yourself, it's somebody else's turn, don't listen, tear out his tongue so he'll stop, cut out his tongue, you don't need to pay a second time*, I thought, *Why should the losers have to bear witness to history — as if being the losers weren't enough, why should the losers have to bear witness to their loss, why should they wear themselves out repeating the story of their loss, and go on repeating it even then, I'm nobody's keeper, it's not fair*, and I thought, without ever saying a word: *No, it's just the opposite of what they say, you should have the right to remain silent, those who have survived violence should have the right to keep it to themselves, they alone should have the right to silence, it's the others whom we should blame for not speaking up*, and Didier wouldn't stop, and Geoffroy backed him up with more and more excitement, more and more conviction, more and more noise, even if he was still the more reserved. I looked down in shame, because of course I was ashamed, and I kept telling myself: *He's forcing me at gunpoint*, and I couldn't say it because I thought they would laugh despite the aptness of the words, and I thought: *They don't want you to get away, all you want is to get away but they're telling you not to move, all you want is to get out of the apartment where you are with Reda, and they don't want you to get out, they don't want you to elbow Reda in the side and get away*; the more they scolded me, the more I felt my throat closing up, my temples throbbed, their words ran down my thighs. And then, in exasperation, after my silence, because I felt I had no choice, I said: 'All right, give me some time to think, let's eat and when we've finished I'll give you an answer, but while we're eating I'd like to talk about something else, let me eat my lunch in peace, if that's not too much to ask.' At the end of the meal, we paid and we walked towards the police station, but my body was not my own, I watched it lead me there.

14

She says the three of us walked into the police station in the place Saint-Sulpice the night of 25 December; she gives her husband the description I gave to her: the garlands of tinsel hanging from the ceiling, the Christmas tree in the corner, the little coloured bulbs blinking green, red, blue, yellow. I'm listening less and less carefully to Clara, her digressions are exhausting.

The officer at the front desk asked how she could help us, but I couldn't speak. My tongue froze in my mouth. Didier answered for me: 'This young man would like to report a crime.' *They've dragged you here by the collar.* She said: 'What's the crime?' *They've dragged you here by the collar and now she's come to join in.* I answered: 'Attempted murder, and rape.' *You didn't see that coming, did you?* She recoiled slightly, as if she might have misheard, she looked at the three of us.

Clara told her husband: 'She was shocked.'

I looked her in the face so she could see I meant it. I looked deep into her eyes. She understood: 'Let me find someone to help you.' The two men standing next to her turned to look at me, having lost all interest in whatever they'd been doing. A policeman came up to me. 'Are you the one?' He raised a hand to Didier and Geoffroy, then smiled at me and asked me to come with him. Didier and Geoffroy were not allowed to come along, they had to wait in that gloomy lobby.

He brought me into his office, he said, 'Have a seat.' He stepped out for a moment and returned. 'Tell me what happened.'

At the beginning he took down what I was saying. Then the tapping of his fingers on the keys grew intermittent. My words came tumbling out. He'd stopped typing altogether, but it took me a while to notice that the sound of the keyboard had trailed off, that it had completely disappeared. Still I went on talking. He interrupted, he said he couldn't take care of 'a case like yours'.

'The crime is too serious, monsieur': he was sending me to another police station, several blocks away though still in the Sixth Arrondissement. I saw myself get up, splinter the door with my shoulder, run down the hallway to the street, and out into the night, and keep running. But there I was, still sitting in the chair, and the policeman was stepping out of the office again.

They explained that I'd have to go in a car. Two men showed up to escort me. I thought of Didier's sweater. The other office where I had to go, they told me, was just down the street, and Didier and Geoffroy would walk over and meet me there. I asked whether I could walk with them – 'That way,' I told Clara, 'I'd have a minute to walk with them and talk to them, I missed them,' and I didn't see why I should have to go in a car. The police had no idea why, either. Those were just their orders, or rather the procedure, they told me they were following procedure, and I thought: *Are procedures there just to be followed, or are procedures there to make things go better?* Sometime later Geoffroy told me that there was a logical explanation for the procedure, and that he'd told me and I'd forgotten.

I hear Clara:

'Both of them short, fat, and bald. Not good-looking at all, not big muscular cops like the ones on TV – as if. Just a couple of stooped little bald guys with pot bellies. He told those two friends of his, Didier and Geoffroy, that the guys by the door were going to take him to the other station because that's where they were making him file the report. And he told them, his friends I mean, "So, I guess that's it. You can go."'

Stop listening. The police had told me that Didier and Geoffroy couldn't be with me in the second police station, that I couldn't see or talk to them, so I told them they could go home. I wasn't thinking, of course, and they're not idiots, so they stayed. They waited in the second police station, which was even bleaker, grimmer and colder than the first. When I walked in, they were there waiting; while I'd been climbing into the car with the two men, while I'd been fastening my seat belt, while the officer was starting the car and releasing the brake, Didier and Geoffroy had already been sitting there, waiting; now Didier was speaking to an officer who wanted me to make an appointment with the psychiatrist for the next day. The police took me upstairs.

At certain moments my anger at Didier and Geoffroy faded, because I was caught up in the chain of events and was no longer thinking of my anger – I even got into the game; in fact, I threw myself into it, whatever the police asked, I answered like the good student I was; after each answer I sat up like a smug A student who expects full marks – shoulders back, eyebrows raised, feeling useful and eager to please – and then the rage would return. Then I snapped out of it, and reminded myself I was there against my will, and the anger would return, but anger is a promise too hard to keep.

'And then they had him tell the whole story all over again.'

They asked me to start over: the police from before hadn't kept any of what they'd written, not even the beginning, not even a few lines. I just wanted to go to sleep. I spent the next month living at Frédéric's apartment, close to both Didier and Geoffroy. I wasn't afraid to sleep at home that first night, but the second night it was impossible – Geoffroy says this is common, this peculiarity about the second night; for some reason people don't feel afraid the first night, only the second;

this was something he heard when he was attending trials for his book on the justice system. Sure enough, when I thought of staying at my own apartment that second night I panicked, and Frédéric invited me to stay at his place for a few months. He said, 'I'm on my way,' and fifteen minutes later he was waiting on the street with a taxi. I had to repeat myself, and repeat myself, all the people around me became pretexts for making me repeat myself, I no longer saw the bodies of men or women, only repetitions that had taken on the bodies of women and men; even so, half an hour later the two officers, the man and the woman, said the same thing that the officer had said at the place Saint-Sulpice, in almost the same words, for they, too, were repeating themselves, and in the same cold, distant, clinical tone: 'We're not authorised to handle a case like yours.' I had to go to yet another office that specialised in these things, I had to see other people, in the Department of Criminal Investigations to be exact, what they called the DCI. I said, 'I can't, I'm too exhausted.' The woman said, 'I understand.' They mulled it over, and she picked up the phone. She told me she'd found a solution, I think she was trying to be reassuring. I waited. They could take my report and forward it to the Department of Criminal Investigations. I wouldn't have to go over it a third time, although I would still have to speak to the DCI later that night, and they'd need to ask me a few more questions, even after they read the report she was going to send them.

I tried to imagine my life over the next few months and all I could see was this process.

I went down the stairs. This time I was determined that Didier and Geoffroy should leave and go home; the female officer had said I could use one of the phones at the police station to let them know what I'd have to do next; all they had to do was write down their numbers on a scrap of paper and I could call them. I tore a sheet out of a promotional booklet, 'The Police Are Recruiting', that was lying around, there were three big stacks of them. Didier and Geoffroy wrote their numbers. The wet ink shone on the glossy paper. Even as they wrote down their numbers, they argued that they should stay. I was firm. In the end they believed me, they thought I wanted them to go. They wouldn't go to bed, they'd wait for me to call. By then it was already quite late, maybe midnight or one.

They walked towards the exit and I watched them go. As soon as they went through the door and disappeared into the night, I felt my organs implode, I wanted to scream but I couldn't make a sound, the air had become unbreathable, my mouth, my throat, my oesophagus, my lungs were imploding, they were shrivelling up, until they felt like crumpled, deflated, veiny bits of rubber. How could I breathe? I wanted to run after them in the street till my legs came unhinged, I wanted to grab them by the arm and drag them back, I wanted to cling to them and beg them to stay and not to listen when I asked them to leave me alone. I made myself cough, just to reassure myself with the sound. If I made a sound, it meant I was still there. For a little while I stood there in the lobby, and for the first time I noticed how cold it was; and from that moment on, that night – like the night before – would be bound up with the memory of being cold.

15

These are all things Clara has heard me tell her over the
last few days, since I came to stay with her: That I had to go
back to the hospital the next day. That the cursory examination I'd had that morning in the emergency room
wasn't enough. That I had to submit to more tests in a
larger hospital that offered a special service, it was called
forensics, but generally known as the FEU, the Forensic
Emergency Unit, where a doctor could confirm the attack,
the beatings and the rest of it, in other words, take the evidence from the traces on my body, which had not been
done the day before at Saint-Louis because I had refused.
Now I simply accepted everything they told me. I was
worn out.

They explained that a medical team at the FEU could
tell precisely whether I had been the victim of an attack
or of attempted murder when I was being strangled,
which would change everything, 'absolutely everything,
monsieur'. By examining and measuring the marks on

my body, they could reveal whether I had crossed that symbolic line, invisible to the non-specialist, that separates a mere wound from near death; as for the forced penetration, they said that, too, would have to be proven: scientifically, with a medical examination.

Clara says the appointment was made over the phone, by a policeman, the night I filed the report at Saint-Sulpice.

Eight hours after they finished questioning me, I found myself in the Forensic Emergency Unit of the Hôtel-Dieu; it was morning. I had crossed Paris the day after a holiday: everything was moving in slow motion, the few cars, the pedestrians, even the incredibly peaceful Seine seemed to be moving in slow motion.

On the walls of the hospital corridor, someone had thumbtacked sheets of paper with the letters 'FEU' and arrows to point the way. I pushed a swing door. I said: 'Am I in the right place?' and I didn't even have to finish asking the question, the nurse at the entrance replied that I was. *She's worked here so long that, just by looking, she can tell why I'm here, why you're here, maybe it's the tone of my voice or the movement of my lips. She could see the entire Christmas Eve unfold before her eyes, all the way from our meeting on the square to my escape, she could see the blue light on our bodies when we were lying down –* or even that other episode I described to Clara the other day, forty-five minutes after we got to my apartment, when Reda and I were lying there out of breath and we heard a sudden noise that startled us both. It came out of nowhere, this noise, and seemed to be right beside us. We were under my thick red blanket, lying there naked; we heard some-one come right up to the door of my apartment – or actually, it was more like we heard someone simply appear at the door. Neither of us moved. We looked at each other. His eyes questioned mine, and my eyes answered that I knew no more than he did. We tried to hold our breath, but that only made our breathing louder and more irregular. The voices on the other side of the door came closer and closer. They were centimetres away from my door; not speaking, but muttering, almost murmuring, we could hear the rustling of the strangers' clothes, the sound of the fabric brushing the mahogany of the door. Reda put his hand on my chest. When I heard what I realised was a key in the lock, my anxiety peaked, the key turned but the door didn't open, and I heard my heart in my ears, I could feel my heart in my eyes as they throbbed behind my eyelids; I thought for a moment and decided it must be Cyril, who had a key to my place and with his usual kindness must have wanted to surprise me, possibly after his Christmas dinner; or maybe he thought I wasn't there and wanted to borrow my place for the night. We listened as the entire tiny mechanism of the lock jammed, the person behind the door was trying to shoulder it open, he kept taking out the key and putting it back in, taking it out and putting it in, he couldn't get the door to open, but he kept push-ing, he wouldn't give up. Now we could clearly make out the voice, it was just one man. I don't know how long this battle lasted, between the man and the door, I don't know how much time passed between that first try with his shoulder and the moment when he realised what had happened and went away laughing, no doubt having come home drunk from a Christmas party and mixed up my door with his own. His voice faded away and he went down the stairs, to which floor I don't know. We couldn't hear. We were laughing too hard ourselves; and in the days to come I would remember moments like these with both terror and nostalgia.

Besides me there were three women in the waiting room, all looking at the floor. When I walked in, they barely looked at me, and immediately, instinctively, I followed their example. I looked away without having to be asked.

Two women were sitting side by side: both thin, pretty, heavily made up. One was wearing thigh-high boots, the other had on shiny red polka-dot flats whose colour matched her lipstick, on purpose I assume. The third woman was very tall; her high heels made her even taller and gave her an arched back; her legs were mannish and hairy, with thick, sturdy, muscular calves. She was wearing a black leather miniskirt and a big coat made of synthetic fur, leopard, which was unbuttoned and hung past her knees. Her hair was short, her beard thick. She was losing her patience with the nurses at the reception desk. I focused on that deep voice of hers, such a contrast to her skirt and her leopard-skin coat. I couldn't help being moved by her beauty, though I tried not to stare, and I suppose the others were doing the same, I think we must all have been watching her discreetly.

'She started yelling,' Clara says. She was warning them, she'd had just about enough: 'Don't you people give a fuck? This is no way to treat a woman, I want to see a doctor and I want to see a doctor now.' She was weeping, her sobs made it impossible to understand what she was saying. And yet I felt safe in that room. I felt at home sitting next to those others. I told myself that we were in the same situation, that they could understand me with more acuity and intelligence than anybody else, which probably isn't true, but my conviction that no one could really *understand* me, an idea that had hounded me since the morning of the twenty-fifth, was suspended as long as I sat there in that room.

Clara lights another cigarette, I hear the click of the lighter, then the long inhalation:

'A nurse came and called him in. When she came into the waiting room, she didn't say his name the way they do at the normal doctor's. She comes up to him and all she does is tap him on the shoulder – like maybe she guessed he didn't want the others to hear his name? I don't know. Maybe she does that with everyone. Anyhow, she guessed. She says his name in his ear. Follow me, she says. She turns and he goes in behind her and the thing is, he told me, he was carrying a copy of the report in his pocket. The cop had printed it the night before, just for him. He'd decided he would just show it to the doctor so he wouldn't have to speak.'

Stop listening. I followed the nurse into the office. I met the doctor, who shook my hand too hard; Clara says doctors always shake hands too hard to show you who's in charge – *Stop listening now*; I sat opposite him, on the other side of his desk.

I handed him the two sheets of paper, as I'd planned. I stood up, I leaned towards him, I took the two-page report from my back pocket and handed it to the doctor, saying, 'I brought you a copy of the report.' He wouldn't look, he barely glanced at the papers. 'I'd rather hear you tell it.' I had nothing to add, and what difference did it make if I spoke. Everything was written down, printed out, right there in front of him on the paper, and I didn't feel like talking. He said again, 'I'd prefer that you told me yourself.' Why? I don't want to talk any more. I thought: *He ought to have asked me to write it down. When I write, I say everything, when I speak I am a coward.* I spoke but my eyes remained dry.

'He couldn't cry. When can't, you can't. He thought about when his grandmother died, when he was a little kid.' What I thought about was Dimitri.

★

It was almost over. They measured and photographed the marks around my neck, the nurse used a long measuring tape like a tailor's. She stretched it over me. She called out the lengths of the marks to the doctor, who wrote them down.

She placed the measuring tape against my skin, it felt cold and rough, and the doctor took some pictures. He talked to himself, for himself: 'I'm going to take one with the flash off, there we go, that's better . . . and one more,' only he didn't say 'there we go', he said 'theeeeeere we go', drawing it out, while the nurse guided him: 'There are some more marks there, and there, and there.' He asked me to lean over, tilt my head, lift one arm, then the other so he could take pictures of all the lesions and not miss any; he pressed here and there, he asked whether it hurt, and how much on a scale from one to ten, and each time I wanted to answer fifteen; what I said was seven or eight. On his desk I saw little framed photos of children skiing, they must have been his children, I hadn't been skiing in a long time. I thought of the scent of peach. They spent a long time on the purple spots around my neck; he told me, 'I can confirm that he must indeed have strangled you quite hard and for quite some time.' The sentence sounded ridiculously pompous, but I told myself: *There was no need for tears, my body was enough.*

He asked me to take off my clothes and instantly I felt the return of my old shame; it was the shame I had felt all my life; even in primary school, check-ups had been an ordeal. So were class trips to the pool: I'd run from one pool to the other, hands clenched over the crotch of my swimsuit and over my penis, curled beneath the fabric; my body sickly and almost deformed; my skin so embarrassingly white, so pale you could see the veins underneath. I undressed as slowly as I could.

The doctor and nurse were both watching and waiting, with no pretence of looking away, and one of them pronounced the inevitable words: 'You can take everything off,' and even knowing those words would be said, even expecting them, did nothing to soften my shock. He told me to get on all fours on the examination table, which was covered with that brown scratchy paper like sandpaper. 'You will feel some discomfort.' He was going to use a spatula to examine the deeper cuts and wounds. Later I told Clara that this was not humiliating, because to admit otherwise would have doubled the humiliation. He pushed the spatula in. He took photographs, *They're photographing the inside of my body.* I heard the little click of the camera every time they took a picture, and the doctor murmuring to the nurse, lesions, haematomas. Clara says he asked me, 'Have you had much bleeding?' I had been bleeding a lot. It would start without any warning. I told the doctor: 'You can't even trust your own blood. It gives you away.' It left stains on my pants. I said: 'If anyone wanted to find me, they could just follow my trail.' He didn't laugh at my joke. He let it go. I felt an urge to laugh. I don't know why I felt like laughing, I made other attempts at humour, each one a failure, each one stupider than the last, and they left a taste of self-loathing in my mouth. I felt inappropriate, vulgar, and he never cracked a smile, but I couldn't stop, each time I made a joke I felt furious with myself, but right away I'd start doing it again. I knew I wasn't being funny, and each time he stiffened even more. At the end of the examination, he recommended that I see a psychiatrist, there was one available in the hospital.

I was sure that if I kept acting like a trauma victim, that's what I'd become – the effects would be even worse and would last longer. Meanwhile my body knew exactly what was going on. I told Clara: there's no way to ignore the blood, there's no way to ignore the fear of being in my apartment. I can't ignore the fatigue that is a side effect of my medication, or the marks on my body, or the way my heart races when I'm walking down the street at night by myself and someone, a man, walks up behind me and I'm scared by the sound of his footsteps. But I knew I had to lie to myself. I don't mean that lying was a solution, and I don't know whether this would work for anyone else, but what I needed was to pretend with all my might that I wasn't traumatised, to tell myself I was all right, even if that was a lie.

It wasn't the first time I was saved by a lie. Looking back, I've often felt most free in moments when I could lie, and by lying I mean resist a truth that was forced on me, on my tissues, on my organs – a truth that was already rooted inside me, that had been rooted inside me for a long time, but that had been planted there by others, that came from without, like the fear that Reda had injected into my body, and I realised that lying was the only power I could call my own, the only weapon I could trust completely. There's a sentence of Hannah Arendt's that I happened to read on the train from Paris, although I haven't repeated it to Clara, who makes fun of me whenever I talk about philosophy; Arendt writes: 'In other words, the deliberate denial of factual truth – the ability to lie – and the capacity to change facts – the ability to act – are interconnected; they owe their existence to the same source: imagination. It is by no means a matter of course that we can *say*, "The sun shines," when it actually is raining . . . ; rather, it indicates that while we are well equipped for the world, sensually as well as mentally, we are not fitted or embedded into it as one of its inalienable parts. We are *free* to change the world and to start something new in it.' That's what saved me – my ability to deny the facts.

Although I'd refused to see a psychiatrist, I had one last appointment – *the very last one*, they promised – with the doctor who would prescribe the rest of my treatment. I preferred to go alone. The corridor that led to the office of this second doctor was illuminated by huge bay windows, and as I walked along I let myself be engulfed by the sunlight, and I thought: *Count down from twelve hundred and it will be over. Twelve hundred. One thousand, one hundred and ninety-nine. One thousand, one hundred and ninety-eight.* The sunbeams poured into the corridor, filling it with blinding light, a light too bright and too pure, a mocking light. I came to the door of the office where they were expecting me. I put my ear to the door to make sure it was my turn, to make sure that, when I opened the door, I wasn't going to interrupt one of the three people I'd met, or rather glimpsed, in the waiting room, talking or weeping with the doctor. All I heard was my own heartbeat in my ear.

I knocked. From the other side of the door the doctor told me to come in. She was tall and thin, with hollow cheeks, a nose that was pinched and bony, and slightly trembling hands – she had the face of a civil servant. She indicated a chair and told me to sit. She spoke very softly, as if it might shatter me if she raised her voice. I thought she was laying it on too thick. She didn't ask many questions, for which I was grateful. She said that what I'd gone through was like a kind of death. On the contrary, I was relieved to have survived and couldn't understand why she'd bring up a thing like death.

Clara rises. I hear her cross the room. She goes to the sink, she fills her water glass. I hear the sound of the water running, the sound of the water filling the glass, the sound of her swallowing when she drinks. She sets the glass down. I hear the chair squeak against the floor as she takes her seat. I'm still behind the door.

'I hate the—'

Stop listening.

Time slowed to a crawl. After I left the doctor's office with my prescription, I wandered on my way to the pharmacy, hoping to kill time and get back to Frédéric's later than if I walked at a steady pace; I didn't want to face an entire day. The pharmacist read what was on the prescription. There was no way he could know that the treatment was only preventive; it didn't say so on the prescription, as far as I know. He gave me a sad, pitying look, the look of an undertaker, and I would have rather he shuddered with disgust than give me that maudlin look.

I walked to Frédéric's. He was in the United States for work and had left me a set of keys. I took the narrowest streets, the longest and most winding, and even so I got there earlier than I wanted. I didn't see how I could have made it back so quickly when I walked so slowly and took so many detours. I collapsed onto the sofa and I thought: *What was my life like before Reda?*

I had gone through all the tests, taken all the mandatory steps, both the official ones, those required by the criminal justice system, and the unofficial – that is, the doctors, the clinical examinations, the police, the Department of Criminal Investigations, the quasi-psychiatric doctors and their advice, and also my own fear, my oscillations between speech and silence, my bursts of self-protective arrogance, as if these, too, were obligatory institutions.

My life was a series of hours. As I told Clara this morning, I couldn't seem to fill up the space left behind when those appointments suddenly came to an end, and it seemed to me unthinkable – unthinkable, and impressive – that for years I'd managed to fill up all the hours of the day from the morning, or at least the afternoon, from whenever I opened my eyes, until evening. I spent my days counting down the hours, I would think, *More than five hours to go before the day ends, more than three hours to go,* I would think, *If I take a long enough shower, that will be half an hour. If you don't brush your teeth in the shower but do it after, you'll waste another three minutes.* If I got out of the shower and saw that it had been less than thirty minutes, I would bite my tongue as punishment, I'd pinch my forearm, and I'd think again: *If you go to the post office and come back at a reasonable pace you'll kill another twenty minutes. Twenty whole minutes, easy;* I used subterfuges, strategies, tricks to trap myself. *What was there before all these appointments, before the taking of statements, before the Hôtel-Dieu?* It's not that I was sorry when the questioning and the medical examinations were over, I didn't miss them; on the contrary, I was relieved; my sense of freedom, now that I could remain silent, or at least stop speaking when I wanted, was like nothing I'd ever felt.

The day began around noon, when I got up; the odd thing was that I never knew how to fill up the day and yet the smallest task, the smallest obstacle, like opening up my laptop, or even just seeing another person, disgusted me – in any case, I hated everyone, just as Clara said. I could spend two or three days in a row sitting on Frédéric's sofa asking myself which was worse, to be bored or to do something I hated; so I didn't do anything. I looked out through his curtains into the courtyard of his building. Although I was agitated, it's not as if time sped up. I never found myself thinking, after some long pointless deliberation, that the time had flown by; on the contrary, my immobility was slow, as if time itself had slowed to a crawl.

After I woke up, I'd spend a few hours in bed, just lying there, or turning over and trying to go back to sleep. The sunlight, coming through the blinds, would reach my face at a certain hour and cover it in warmth that left me feeling even more listless and oppressed.

I wouldn't exactly sleep: I would doze, and even as I dreamed I would retain a vague sense that I wasn't actually asleep. Sometimes, when I was in that space between reality and dreams, I could have sworn I was able to change the things that happened in my dreams. I was dreaming, but inside the dream I knew that I was dreaming, and I could modify the landscape, I could make certain people appear around me and make others disappear, and nothing could frighten me, I could jump off a cliff, off the sixtieth floor of a high-rise, or burn down a forest just to admire the mysterious beauty of its destruction: if something bad happened, I'd wake myself up and I'd be alone again, in my bed.

The individual I had become would carefully place the three pills of his antiretroviral medication on a sheet of newspaper spread out next to him in the bed, where it remained all night. Then, when he woke up, he would take his medication. He would have cut the pills into little pieces the night before so he could swallow them more easily in the morning. This routine allowed him to stay in bed, so he didn't have to get up and go to the medicine cabinet. He kept a bottle of water in the bed, next to him on the mattress, all night long, and he would tuck it in as if it were his child, and now and then it would roll against his body and wake him up, when he felt the coolness of the water in the bottle against his back. He left it there to wash down the big pills of Kaletra and Truvada, since even when he took them separately, broken into two or three pieces, they were still painful to swallow and scratched his oesophagus. If he had forgotten to put his bottle of water in the bed beside him the night before, he would take his pills without water rather than get out of bed, and for hours he'd feel them stuck somewhere between his gut and the back of his mouth. He'd swallow over and over, trying to make them go down, but he was only swallowing air and he'd burp it up again; he'd try to bring them down into his body by contracting his throat and oesophagus.

And yet the doctor had warned him: under no circumstances should he take his medicine on an empty stomach, not unless he had breakfast right after. And in fact, very often, when he took his pills on an empty stomach, the first thing he did was limp to the toilet so he could throw up, holding his hands out before him like a bad actor imitating a blind man, still between sleep and waking, eyes squinted shut, mouth gummy from sleep. The acid odour of the vomit would wake him. He hoped this didn't interfere with the treatment, he hoped the pills had had time to dissolve in his stomach and spread through his tissues and bloodstream between the time he'd swallowed them and the moment when he found himself on his knees against the toilet, leaning over the bowl, hands firmly planted on the plastic seat – because he was afraid of drowning in the toilet bowl, drowning in the water and the rejected contents of his stomach, and his body would be racked with spasms, and there would be nothing left to throw up since he hadn't eaten, and his body would contract, arch and twist the way you wring out a damp rag to squeeze out the last drops of water. Even if he didn't throw up, the nausea would persist from morning to night. Often he took a nap in the afternoon. He'd get up at noon, wander around the apartment, then go back to bed at two, get up at six, and nervously wait for dark so he could go back to bed again. He had to follow the course of treatment, his body didn't tolerate it well, and since it began his nights had stretched from eight hours to fifteen or sixteen hours per day, and the whole time he kept thinking, *After all you've been through.*

He would plan little returns to normal life. He secretly called these his sorties. He liked to make up code names, code expressions to use in his communications with himself; he never shared these communications, he never told anyone about them but kept them jealously private; he would murmur to himself, 'Today it's time to make another sortie.' And he would leave the apartment. He would force himself to go. He would go down to the café and spy on the others around him. He would go to the café wearing an old hoodie, the oldest he had, one that was frayed and full of holes. He wouldn't take a shower. He'd yank his hood down over his dirty, greasy hair. He dressed as badly as he could, thinking, *I want to look the way I feel, I want to be as repulsive as the thing that happened to me.*

There was something else, too.

I had become racist. Suddenly I was full of racism – the one thing I had always considered most alien, most 'other' to my mind. Now I became one of those others. I became exactly the thing I had always rejected becoming – because you don't become anything without excluding other possibilities, and now one of those possibilities had reared up from my past.

A second person took over my body; he thought for me, he spoke for me, he trembled for me, he was afraid for me, he inflicted his fear on me, he made me tremble over terrors of his own. On the bus or the metro I lowered my eyes if a man who was black or Arab or possibly Kabyle came anywhere near me – because it was always men, and this was another absurd feature of the racist fantasy that colonised my being: the danger always came in the shape of a man. I would lower my eyes or turn my head and silently beg, *Don't attack me, don't attack me.* I never bowed my head if the man was blond or red-headed, or if he had very pale skin.

I was traumatised twice over: by fear and by my fear.

This lasted two or three months.

There was Istanbul. Cyril had invited me to come with him to Turkey just after Christmas. I hesitated. I didn't know if it was a good idea, and one day when I went for my blood tests at the Hôtel-Dieu I asked the nurse what she thought. She'd said: 'It will do you good to get away a few days and clear out the cobwebs.'

I flew to Turkey with Cyril. I slept in my seat on the plane. Only I didn't sleep, I pretended to sleep so I wouldn't have to talk. I did it all very carefully: I pretended to wake up when the wheels of the plane touched down, I stretched my arms, I rubbed my eyes, I yawned, I inhaled and exhaled voluptuously, as if I were waking from a dream. From the moment I set foot in Istanbul, at the airport, I counted the days until it was time to leave. Immediately I realised what a mistake it had been to come on this trip; I multiplied the number of days by twenty-four to get the number of hours I'd have to spend there. I multiplied the total by sixty using the calculator on my phone to figure out the number of minutes I'd have to stay. I started counting.

I saw menace everywhere. Whenever Cyril looked at me, I felt sure he was about to discover the contemptible, shameful reason for my fear. I hid my face so no one could read my features. The city amplified everything I was afraid of: the call to prayer, echoing through the streets, chanted my impending doom; the sun had been invented to burn my face, the pressing crowd that jostled along the great pedestrian artery existed to crush and trample me, the world was a production staged against me. I tried to keep Cyril from seeing that I felt safer when I walked beside someone I took to be a white American or white German. I walked closer to them, thinking they would protect me in case of an attack; and I was disgusted with myself. But I did it.

Even in the taxi from the airport, my paranoia had invented all kinds of scenarios. The driver glanced at us through the rear-view mirror and asked us questions about our lives, our jobs, France. Cyril answered for me, and each time he opened his mouth I braced myself, thinking he was about to go too far, that he'd give something away that would offend the driver. I kept shooting him stern looks full of hatred. He didn't notice, he was too absorbed with the taxi driver, since he's always eager to meet new people and talk with strangers. I saw the driver take us on a long trip, over crumbling and inter-minable roads, to the edge of a forest of sunburned trees. The trees weren't brown or green, but yellow, dry, incandescent, as if they were on fire from root to branch. The driver took us there, we asked him to take us to the hotel and he took us to this forest, and I knew what he had planned, but Cyril was smiling, oblivious, and he kept talking to the driver and saying things he shouldn't say. I wanted to warn him, but in my vision I didn't warn him, because I was afraid it would hasten the inev-itable. Then he realised. But now it was too late. The driver stopped the car. He forced us to get out, he ordered us in broken English, *Go off, go outside the car,* first calmly, then more and more nervously, until it sounded like a furious insult, *Go out,* then he opened the door to get us out faster, and he kicked us, and finally he pulled out a gun that looked like Reda's, that was exactly the same, in the dream I recognised it perfectly. Then he shot us. Nothingness. The driver had dropped us in front of the hotel, and I had given him a large tip.

16

For the first time he speaks. He says: 'I better get going, they'll be waiting for me.' She answers: 'Let me finish, I'm almost done,' and it's true, just now her voice had the sound of someone wrapping up; even though I've been listening less and less, for some time now I've known she was nearing the end.

The night of my second interview with the two police officers, before I left, the female officer told me that four men would be waiting in front of my building. They were on their way now, they'd be taking fingerprints so they could, in the end, perhaps, find Reda. I called Geoffroy. Didier was supposed to avoid moving around because he had a bad back, he'd spent too much time that winter at his computer, writing; Geoffroy said he'd catch a taxi and meet me at home. It was almost two in the morning.

The police car took me back to my apartment. Through the car window I could see the revolving blue lights.

There were two men with me. They didn't put on the radio. We came to the place de la République, they said good night; I walked a short way in the dark, I passed the pulled-down metal gates of the cafés, and soon I saw the shapes of the four men standing in front of my building, each one carrying a little aluminium suitcase. They were dressed in dark colours, parkas, jeans, a couple in trainers, a couple in leather shoes. Just like on TV, I thought. I went nearer. I walked up to them, they peered into my face, frowning, I asked: 'Are you with Criminal Investigations?' and one of them answered, 'Yes, and you are Monsieur—' And I interrupted, 'Yeah, that's me.'

'He didn't know what else to say,' Clara says. I just walked up to the door and punched in the security code and they followed. They took pictures of the door before we went upstairs; they took dozens and dozens of snapshots, the camera kept clicking away, they were talking back and forth but I couldn't understand a word of what they were saying, I couldn't see why they'd need a picture of this blue front door with its flaking paint when Reda never even touched it, or why they'd take a picture of my mailbox, which Reda had never even noticed – at least I don't think he did, if so I don't remember; he wouldn't have been able to tell it apart from the others because I don't remember having told him my last name – or why they'd take such an interest in the elevator when Reda had never been inside it, but I didn't ask any questions, I didn't want this to take any longer than it had to. Geoffroy must have been somewhere between his house and mine; in any case he wouldn't be long. They asked questions and more questions: 'Did he touch the intercom? The front door? Did he touch the intercom with his fingers? How about the front door?' I said no, he hadn't touched any of those things, I was the one who punched in the code, I was the one who invited him in, I was the one who wanted him in my home; and they kept taking pictures of my staircase, where nothing in particular had happened, or of the place they kept the dustbins, which Reda had never even seen. Geoffroy would be there soon.

We went up the stairs. I climbed them two by two, and they followed. I can't remember whether they said anything or not. They opened their metal cases in my apartment, having set them down on the floor. These were filled with equipment I couldn't identify. The inspector, the one who spoke the most and had introduced himself as the inspector, was the one giving the orders. He was giving instructions to his team when Geoffroy knocked at the door. It wasn't quite closed, it swung open when he knocked, and he apologised. He put his head round the door and coughed, the inspector looked at him then at me, then me, then him, and asked me if I knew him. Even before I answered, I think he could tell that I'd been expecting Geoffroy – as my sister says, I don't exactly have a poker face. The inspector said Geoffroy couldn't stay, he'd have to wait until they left.

He said: 'We have to be able to do our jobs right, monsieur, I'm sorry,' and he really seemed to mean it, as he went on to remark on the size of the apartment, saying it was too small, it was tight even for five people, which made it hard to look for prints. But Geoffroy would stay on the sofa, he wouldn't move. I begged the inspector: he wouldn't speak, he wouldn't make any noise. It was Geoffroy who settled it, saying he didn't want to get in their way and he'd wait on the landing until they finished, the same landing where I'd seen Reda for the last time the night before. He sat there on the steps, though he had to get up every seventy or eighty seconds to turn on the light, which went off automatically. Clara, who's telling this to her husband, doesn't know it, but after a while he'd had enough and resigned himself to darkness. He stopped getting up, he just sat there in the pitch black. I couldn't hear him any more.

They questioned me; they wanted to know where they might be able to find fingerprints; and they thought of the sheets, but I'd washed them all, and the clothes, too, I'd washed those at the highest temperature. I'd thrown my trousers and my underwear away in a public dustbin when I was on my way from my place to Henri's. All I had was my shirt and sweater, but they weren't any use, there were no prints on them, I'd taken them off myself five minutes after Reda got there, and he'd hardly touched them.

The only fingerprints they could find were on the

vodka bottle – but had Reda touched it? I couldn't remember, I didn't think so – and on the pack of cigarettes that had fallen out of his pocket when he got dressed. The bottle was still in the dustbin downstairs where I'd put it that morning. And I hadn't washed the glass he drank from, either. I have no idea why, but when I'd scrubbed every centimetre of the place to exorcise his presence from my apartment, I hadn't done the dishes and I hadn't washed the glass he'd drunk from, and this was something I didn't realise until I was back at home with the men from Criminal Investigations. I'd washed everything, I'd used bleach and anything else I could find; to me the stink of the bleach was reassuring, but the glass where he'd put his lips remained untouched, and the most incredible thing, more incredible even than the glass, was that I'd left his pack of cigarettes on the floor – that, and a pocket dictionary that had fallen out of his clothes. I'd tried to get rid of every trace of him, I'd washed the floor, but somehow I'd worked around the pack of cigarettes and the pocket dictionary, lying there side by side; you could actually see where I'd mopped. I'd made a circle around the pocket dictionary and the cigarettes and you could clearly see this circle of darker parquet in the middle of the clean, freshly washed parquet, and in this circle, at its centre, the two objects, which hadn't been moved by so much as a centimetre. *You'd overlooked them, even though you washed the slats of the blinds one by one, the blinds he'd never touched, you polished the doorknobs, you emptied whole bottles of bleach into the toilet but you left the pack of cigarettes and the dictionary. There they are, in the middle of the room, and you'd overlooked them.* The inspector asked me why I'd left the cigarettes and the dictionary sitting there, under the chair, but I didn't know what to say. He suggested that I go downstairs and look in the rubbish for the vodka bottle. Geoffroy smiled as I went past. I had no trouble finding the plastic bag; there it was, untouched, wrapped in the odours of rotten fruit and the stink of dirty nappies. *Two four six eight.* I counted the stairs as I climbed them. I gave the bag to the policemen, they extracted the bottle slowly, using just the tips of their fingers. They were wearing plastic gloves. They used a special powder that they spread over the bottle with what looked like a shaving brush. They couldn't find any prints. They found a couple of smudges but they said those were illegible and almost certainly wouldn't yield any information, they might not have belonged to Reda anyway. All that was left was the glass, unbelievably left where it was, and the pack of cigarettes and the little book. They didn't find any prints on the glass either, or on the cigarette pack, which surprised Geoffroy afterwards, though I didn't think about it at the time, I was too tired to be surprised by anything. Their voices said the prints weren't in good enough condition. In my heart I prayed they wouldn't find anything. I was helpful, just as I'd been helpful at Saint-Sulpice, I helped them look for clues, I went down to the rubbish bins to get the bag, I answered their questions, I cooperated; I didn't say the bag was gone, which would have been simple enough; but then suddenly I'd pull myself together and start inventing memory lapses – to say either that I was a participant in what happened or else that I resisted would be equally true and false; neither version would capture the reality. They stayed an hour and during that hour I had as many contradictory feelings as they had questions.

I'm not listening to Clara any more.

They spread out into every corner of the apartment, their trainers squeaking on the floor, which was still sticky from all the cleaning products I'd used that morning. In several places they sprinkled black powder – on the cigarette pack, on the metal bed frame, on the dishes. First they'd pour it out, then they'd use little clear adhesive strips which, together with the powder, would make fingerprints appear. The powder would sit there, untouched by me, for more than a month, since it was early the next day when I went to stay at Frédéric's. When I came back to the studio in February there was black powder everywhere, as if a storm of ash or charcoal had swept in while I was away.

Another policeman used cotton swabs and a liquid product to take DNA samples from the rim of the glass Reda had used. 'It won't be easy, the sample isn't very good, I'm not getting much, oh, but wait, there's a good one, yeah, I think that one's going to work . . .' While they were looking for fingerprints, I sat waiting on the bed. They'd already finished with that part of the studio, and now and then I'd go out to Geoffroy on the landing and apologise for making him wait. He lied: 'It's no problem at all, I'm very comfortable out here.' The inspector asked me to stop going outside, he said he needed me to stay put.

I went back and sat on the bed. I didn't even have my phone so I could pretend to read my messages.

They'd finished their work and were getting ready to leave. The inspector apologised for all the black powder on the dishes and everything. It didn't matter, it was all right, I was going to clean up anyway. I wanted to roll in that black powder. The cases were all packed up; they said good night, they shook my hand and went out the door. Just as they were leaving and Geoffroy was getting up to come into the apartment, they asked whether Reda had taken a shower, since then they might find some prints on the shower partition or the bottle of liquid soap; and I didn't lie. I don't know why not, but I didn't lie, I said yes, and because of me they turned round. They went into the bathroom, where they spent another ten minutes. Time dragged by. Ten minutes later they left for good, but not before one of them asked, for the last time, 'You're sure there's nowhere else we could look?'

Now Geoffroy could join me inside the apartment. He sat down on the bed next to me, and neither of us could think of anything to say. This never happened with us, at least it had never happened before; very often, in fact, we talked too much when we were together, we were liable to interrupt each other, our words would pile up or collide, in the space of a breath one phrase would find its way inside another and explode it and jolt the conversation into an entirely new direction. But that night, alone in the apartment reeking of bleach, we had nothing to say. No noise came up from the courtyard, there was nothing but silence and the smell of detergent.

He said: 'You must want to get some sleep.' That, too, he'd understood, but I hadn't had the courage to say it. I hadn't had the courage to tell him to go home and leave me alone after he'd spent an hour, maybe longer, on the landing, in the dark, sitting there on the cold stairs. 'You're not afraid to stay here by yourself?' No, I wasn't afraid. I couldn't manage more than three or four words at a time. I wanted to be alone. I told him again: 'No, I'm not afraid.' He told me he could stay beside me and wait until I fell asleep. Once I had, he would leave without a sound, he would sneak out, on tiptoe, without banging the door, and the next day he'd come back with Didier.

It turned out that it is impossible to write about happiness, or at least I can't, which in this case amounts to the same thing after all; happiness is perhaps too simple to let itself be written about, I wrote, as I am reading right now on a slip of paper that I wrote then and from which I am writing it down here; a life lived in happiness is therefore a life lived in muteness, I wrote. It turned out that writing about life amounts to thinking about life, and thinking about life amounts to casting doubt on life, but only one who is suffocated by his very lifeblood, or in whom it somehow circulates unnaturally, casts doubt on that lifeblood. It turned out that I don't write in order to seek pleasure; on the contrary, it turned out that by writing I am seeking pain, the most acute possible, well-nigh intolerable pain, most likely because pain is truth, and as to what constitutes truth, I wrote, the answer is so simple: truth is what consumes you, I wrote.

Imre Kertész,
Kaddish for an Unborn Child